THE SERPENT
AND
THE SORCERESS

To Jordyn—

There is a dragon in us
all. If we learn to control
that dragon we will be
powerful indeed.

Yours in writing!

Nan Whybark

November 2011

THE SERPENT AND THE SORCERESS

Book 2, Earth to Irth series

Nan Whybark

iUniverse, Inc.
Bloomington

THE SERPENT AND THE SORCERESS
BOOK 2, EARTH TO IRTH SERIES

iUniverse books may be ordered through booksellers or by contacting:

iUniverse
1663 Liberty Drive
Bloomington, IN 47403
www.iuniverse.com
1-800-Authors (1-800-288-4677)

ISBN: 978-1-4620-5447-3 (sc)
ISBN: 978-1-4620-5448-0 (ebk)

Printed in the United States of America

iUniverse rev. date: 10/06/2011

CHAPTER 1

Full of excitement, Princess Krystin burst into the royal bed chambers. "Mother! What do you think about this dress?" She held up a delicate, pale blue taffeta gown with flowing ribbons and satin sleeves. "Isn't it just the most beautiful thing you've ever seen?" she cried. "Do you think it will do for the visit of the Duke and Duchess of Northford?"

Prince David (the title seemed unnatural to him) frowned as he walked past the open doorway. He was bored with life in the castle. He hated the servants who fussed about his clothes, his manners, his speech, and where he should stand and when he should sit and how to bow. He hated the stuffy, scholarly teacher his parents had arranged for his formal education. Everything had to be proper and just so. It was suffocating him. He longed for the freedom of the old forest home.

David paused and glanced back as his sister, Krystin, fluttered back into the hall with their Mother. Krystin had taken to castle life with vigor. She loved all the attention and finery. She loved all the formalities and the people. She glowed with excitement whenever there was visiting royalty or diplomats from other cities. She was full of questions and eager to know of other places and people.

In the last five years, David had grown to be much taller than his sister. In fact he was only just shorter than his father, King Stephon and his brother, Crown Prince Eron.

But Krystin had enough energy to be twelve feet tall. Her green eyes sparkled with life and curiosity, and she laughed often. She adored her tutor and longed for more books to read when she wasn't swooning over some handsome stranger at a royal gathering. She now kept her long, golden brown hair braided and hanging down her back, or pinned up like Mother's. She looked for any opportunity to crown her head with the circlet of gold she had been given as sole princess of the kingdom of Lyndell.

David shook his head and looked over at his mother, Aryanne. He had always thought she was pretty, even in a simple peasant dress and apron. But in her royal satins and velvets, she was a regal beauty. Her long, brown-black hair, touched with white at the temples, was pinned up. A few unruly wisps played about her face. Her high cheekbones, slender straight-bridged nose and pale skin gave her the air of divinity. Her eyes were the color of the summer sky, and just as bright and warm. David had to admit that Krystin, even though she had father's coloring, was looking more like their mother every day.

Krystin had taken a special liking to one of the royal knights in their father's personal guard. Also there was a certain prince that had been quite taken with Krystin last winter when his passing caravan had to stay an extra week due to a storm. The prince's letters and gifts had never ceased after he had gone. Krystin loved the romance of it all.

Now with spring in the air and Krystin being nearly sixteen years old, David sensed a wedding was likely in the near future. More pomp and ceremony! David shook his head at the thought of it. The castle would be swarming with servants and guests! He needed to get away!

Turning, he hurried on toward the throne room where he knew his father would be conducting the last of the kingdom's business of the day. There would be a break before the king would start receiving visitors and villagers' requests and complaints. David hoped to speak to his father during this break. He had an idea he hoped his father would approve.

He continued toward the throne room, still frowning as he thought about all that had happened since his family had moved back to the castle.

Five years had passed since he and his older sister, Krystin, had gone off on a daring rescue mission to save a talking weasel from Zarcon, a wicked wizard. They had not only made the rescue, but had found Eron, the older brother they never knew they had, and reunited their family. They had been separated and threatened by Zarcon for ten years.

David and Krystin had been stunned to then discover that they, along with their parents, were royalty. Their parents had resumed their roles and rightful place back in the castle.

Word had been sent to the east and north about the return of the king and the disposal of the wizard. The people of the kingdom of Lyndell that were left, along with others, slowly returned and rebuilt the now thriving community of Dayn. Trade with neighboring towns and kingdoms increased almost daily. Life was becoming more crowded, more complicated, and more to David's disliking.

CHAPTER 2

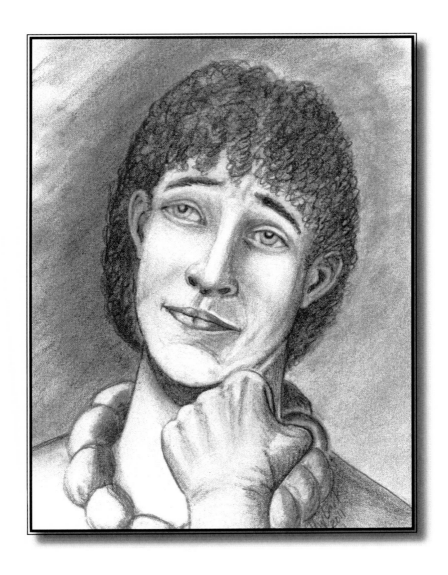

The prince's timing was good. He slipped into the back of the throne room just as the king's advisors stood, gave their salute of allegiance, and were dismissed. David skirted the edge of the crowd and came up just behind his father and the King's First Advisor, Willier, as the posted guard was opening the rear door that led to the king's private chamber and council room behind the raised throne.

King Stephon was a good man. His tall, slender frame was crowned with graying, golden-brown hair which brushed his broad shoulders. His mind was sharp and wise, and showed in the glint and sparkle of his green eyes. He was an excellent king too, and always busy now with affairs of the kingdom and the training of his oldest son, Eron, who would someday take his place as king of Lyndell. The king had no more time for hunting trips.

David missed the closeness and attention he had so readily received from his father when they had been exiled in the forest cottage. It was a simpler life then, even if it was harder work. He had enjoyed the work and the struggle to live. Those times were before he even knew he had a brother. Even though Eron was 10 years older than David, he had enjoyed the new relationship. But like his father, Eron was soon caught up in the business of the kingdom, leaving David feeling left out and alone.

The king and Willier were deep in discussion and neither of them noticed as David went with them into the council room. Stephon moved to the large, heavily draped windows. "Blast these drapes!" the king erupted, looking up suddenly. "We finally get some warming to the weather and some light in the sky and the servants still never open the draperies! It's like a dungeon in here!"

"I'll see to it at once, your majesty!" Willier quickly responded and, turning on his heel, hurried out of the room. David snatched the opportunity to capture his father's attention.

"Father, I . . ."

"Ah, David! There you are! Have you been practicing your swordplay?"

"Yes, but I wanted to . . . ."

"And how are your studies going? If you are to be my foreign minister someday, you must be up on your studies of world affairs and trade."

"Father, I want to talk to you about a hunting trip."

"Hunting trip? David, you know that's out of the question right now. I've got Duke Berril coming tomorrow to talk over a land dispute in Northford, and King Vandenor two days after that to discuss an alliance against the barbaric tribes in the southern waste. With your brother, Eron, on a diplomatic mission until next month I can't possibly go now.

"But, Father, I . . ."

"No sense discussing it further, Son." the king hurried on.

"But, I didn't mean that you . . ."

"Where is that confounded Willier?" Stephon moved back toward the nearest window. "Shall I be forced to rip down these stifling draperies myself?"

David could feel his own anger and frustration rising into his throat. He wanted to scream and he did.

"PERMISSION TO SPEAK TO HIS ROYAL HIGHNESS!" he bellowed at his father's back.

The king whirled around, anger darkening his face. David stood stiff with his own anger, facing his father. There were several long seconds that passed in silence before his father relaxed and his face softened. The king shook is head sadly. "I'm sorry, David," he said quietly as he walked forward and placed a hand on his son's shoulder. "It's just not the same anymore, is it?"

David looked at the lines in his father's face and his graying hair. Moving back to the castle and regaining his place as king had taken a heavy toll on his father. David sighed as his anger dissolved into sadness. "It will <u>never</u> be the same again, will it?" He looked into his father's eyes.

"No, David, I'm afraid it will not. Now, what did you want to tell me?"

David took a deep breath and said, "Father, I want to go on a hunting trip." Then seeing his father about to object again, he hurried on, "I know you have no time to go, so I want to go alone."

Stephon opened his mouth to respond, but David cut him off. "I can do it! I'm 14 now. I'll just stay at the old cottage and be back in a few days."

The king stroked his chin. His eyebrows angled down as he frowned and considered his son's proposal. Finally he said, "All right, but I'll send Sir Edgar with you."

"I want to go alone," David protested. "I <u>need</u> to go alone. Please!"

David was surprised when his father's serious face changed to smiling and then erupted in a hearty laugh. "I know just what you mean! I envy you the chance to get away from all this. Some time alone in the peace and simplicity of the forest would be a welcome break for me too. I was gallivanting all over the countryside and hunting alone at your age." He clapped David on the back. "Very well, my son. Go. Take a sturdy horse and adequate provisions. Perhaps when Eron returns I can leave matters to him for a few days and escape myself."

"Thank you, Father!" David replied, smiling broadly.

"Be back within the week or the queen will have my head!"

The king dropped his voice to a whisper, "And don't say a word to your mother. You know how she is. Just go." He laughed again, winking at his son. "I'll tell her when the time is right."

Willier bustled into the room with several servants who all bowed then attacked the heavy draperies, pulling and tugging them to the sides of the windows. "Now about that new provision for the poor, Your Highness," Willier began, turning the king aside.

Seeing his moment with his father was over, David retreated quickly out of the room toward the kitchen and stables, making sure, as his father suggested, to stay clear of the queen.

CHAPTER 3

He was free! David kicked his horse to a gallop before he even reached the portcullis. Ducking his head to clear the heavy, iron gate, he nearly knocked several guards off the drawbridge into the moat. He laughed out loud as the guards' curses followed him down the road and out into the broad meadow beyond. He was glad the town had built up to the north and east of the castle so that the meadow and forest on the opposite side were still untouched. He could be well away from the castle and out of sight in the heavily forested hills almost instantly.

He couldn't stop smiling.

David reined in his horse at the edge of the meadow and looked back momentarily, remembering the first time he had seen the castle. It seemed a lifetime ago when he and Krystin had come to rescue the talking weasel. He frowned slightly. Sometimes he wished they had never found the castle. It had changed his life so completely, so miserably.

His horse stirred anxiously under him. David reached down to pat its neck. "You're right, boy," he said. "Let's not waste time with unhappy thoughts. Adventure awaits! And there's no one to tell us what to do!" David laughed out loud. He spun his horse toward the trees and trotted into the shadows of the forest.

The trip from the cottage to the castle with Krystin on foot so long ago had taken them three days, but on horseback with a good knowledge of the way, the time would be considerably less. He would spend one night in the open and the next in the comfort of the cottage. He hoped there was still a stack of firewood in back of the place. There might even be some vegetables that had self-seeded in his mother's garden, now abandoned to the wild.

He pictured the old place in his mind as his horse plodded along the forest path. The main floor of the cottage had only two rooms. One was a large L-shaped room that was both kitchen and sitting room, and the other a tiny room in the back corner that had been his parent's bedroom.

In the opposite corner, there was a loft over the sitting room where he and Krystin had slept as children. It had been the warmest place in the cottage on cold winter nights, and unfortunately, also on hot summer evenings.

The front door opened to the great room on the sitting side and the narrow back door opened from the kitchen out to the garden, shed, coop and wood piles. The kitchen had a large stone fireplace for cooking with an oven built in for baking. There was a small table where the food was prepared and the family sat to eat. The sitting room also had a fireplace, but smaller and just right for cozying up to in one of Father's handmade chairs as he told tall tales of ogres, dragons and brave knights.

David grimaced as he remembered. Ogres and dragons! He shook his head. He'd certainly make an effort to avoid all that nonsense. It was Mr. Weasel who had gotten him into this whole mess in the first place. David was not eager to encounter him again, not to mention Glurb, the swamp monster. David would be very careful to stay clear of the swamp this time. Even though Glurb had proven to be helpful, David still was not completely comfortable with magical or enchanted creatures.

The rest of the day passed by uneventfully, which was just the way David liked it. He breathed the pine-scented air and listened to the chatter of birds playing tag in and out of the trees and bushes. His horse walked on steadily and David didn't hurry it along. It was the journey, not just the destination, he wanted to enjoy. Maybe he would spend the second night in the forest just for fun.

As the sun dipped behind the treetops, the forest air grew moist and chill. David found a protected spot to camp for the night and built a fire. He ate a filling meal of dried meat, biscuits, some crisp spring greens, and a sweet apple he baked in the fire's coals. Then he sat back to watch the flickering flames and dancing sparks. This, and the music of crickets and peeper frogs, was all the entertainment he needed.

He was happier than he had been for months as he lounged under the towering pines, catching a glimpse of the star-filled sky overhead. The prince felt the pressures of castle life drift away like the smoke from the fire. When he became drowsy, he piled more wood on the fire to keep the wild animals at bay, rolled up in his blankets and slept deeply.

The morning was cold and damp as was usual for spring. But the clear sky promised the warming of the sun. After a quick bread-cake cooked on the remaining coals from last night's fire and a refreshing splash and drink from a nearby stream, David was astride his horse and on his way again. He would be at the cottage by late afternoon. His thoughts quickly turned to hunting. It would be a shame to waste such a glorious day without a bit of hunting, and a pheasant or rabbit would be a welcome dinner.

After riding for a couple of hours, David dismounted and twisted his horse's reins around the branches of a low bush. He retrieved his bow and quiver of arrows from a satchel and, walking on, left the horse to graze contentedly.

The young prince hoped to startle some game out of the bushes and be ready for the kill. His quiet padding was rewarded as a flurry of wings erupted out of the brush. His aim was quick and accurate and he got away two shots. After a short search, he discovered his arrows had found their marks. David tied the two fat quail to his saddle pack.

Now he just needed to gather a few fresh herbs and wild onions and he'd eat like a king. *Like a king?* He laughed out loud. No, there would be no servants, no pestering maids bending over him and fussing. Tonight he would eat like a poor man, and that was fine with him.

Anxious now to arrive at the cottage with his prize, David mounted his horse and trotted on. He stood in the stirrups as he grew near, straining for the first glimpse. But he didn't need to squint to see that there was smoke coming out of the chimneys. He reined his horse in and quickly dismounted, running silently the last few yards to the hedgerow of bushes just at the edge of the overgrown front yard. Being careful to keep himself concealed, he peered at the cottage. He saw a dark figure pass the window. Someone was in there.

CHAPTER 4

David backed up silently to where he had tethered his horse and stood there thinking. *What should he do? What could he do?* Now that he thought about it, it wasn't surprising that someone had moved into the cottage. After all, it had been five years since his family had abandoned it. They had made a few trips back to gather things they could not take on the first trip. And early on, he, and Eron and their father had come to stay a few days on some hunting trips. That was before the kingdom had begun to flourish and demand the king's full attention.

But he was the king's son and prince of Lyndell. He could order the occupant to get out. He could say it was by order of the king. Or he could just turn around and spend his few days in the forest, but he had so looked forward to spending the time at his old home. Besides, his curiosity was aroused. Who was in the cottage? Certainly his father would want to know. The king liked to know everything.

That decided it. David would go up to the cottage and find out who was in there. Perhaps it was just a wandering youth he could bully out or at least bunk with. Perhaps it was an old trapper wintering over, waiting for the weather to warm a bit more.

David decided he would keep his identity to himself. There could be more than one in the cottage and they may not be at all friendly. It might be safer if he were just another traveler seeking shelter for the night.

He mounted his horse and clucked it forward at a leisurely walk. When he reached the clearing in front of the cottage he dismounted again and tied the reins in the hedgerow. He left his bow and quiver, but kept his hunting knife on his belt just in case.

He walked casually up to the front door and rapped loudly. The birds and peepers became still at the sudden sound. David looked around at the forest behind him in the eerie quiet. When he turned around again the door was open and he was face to face with the cottage resident. He nearly stumbled backward in surprise! It was a girl!

Actually, it was a young woman, perhaps his own age or a little older. Her pale face was lit by luminous green eyes and surrounded by flames of wavy red hair that hung to her waist. She was several inches shorter than him and dressed in a long, loose, deep blue robe that had shimmering points of light on it like stars. David thought he had seen that type of cloth before, but couldn't get his mind to focus as he stared, open-mouthed, into those bright green eyes. The spell was finally broken when she spoke to him.

"Can I help you?" she asked. Her voice was like a cool breeze on his face, refreshing him, relaxing him, making him long for more. David felt his strength giving way. He shook himself.

"Um . . . . no . . . . I mean, yes . . . . I mean . . . ," David fumbled on, "Do you live here?"

Her eyes narrowed a bit, but she continued her steady gaze at him. "Yes, what brings you here?"

David was having difficulty thinking, his mind seemed foggy. "I, um . . . . was looking for a place to stay the night . . . . but I . . . ," he stopped mid-sentence as she smiled at him.

"You are welcome to stay here," she said without hesitation. She took David's arm and walked him into the cottage, closing the door behind them.

David felt like he was moving in slow motion. He let himself be led into the sitting room by a stranger, and he sat down heavily in a chair. He felt slightly dizzy. The girl looked away from him, distracted by a movement in the kitchen area, and David found his head clearing a bit.

"My name is David," he said. "I'm out hunting and have gone too far to return home tonight. There might be a storm coming. I saw your chimney smoke."

She had moved several steps away into the kitchen. She was turned away from him, her thick hair cascading down her back, as she cooed to a small, white bird, captive in a hanging cage. "I am Odethia," she stated without turning around. "I'm a stranger in this land, but when I found this cottage, I stayed." She turned slowly to stare at David again. Her eyes seemed to glow in the dimly lit room. "Let me fix you a drink and perhaps you can tell me more about this country and its people." Odethia smiled sweetly, and then busied herself making some tea.

Free from her penetrating eyes once more, David's mind focused. He must be on guard, though she seemed harmless enough. He found his own eyes kept wandering back to her as he looked over the familiar room.

There were a few changes, but the place had been kept clean and he could see some new thatch added to the kitchen ceiling. There were bunches of dried herbs hanging from the rafters and walls throughout most of the sitting room. Jars of powders, berries and liquids were strewn all over the kitchen table and shelves. It seemed to David that Odethia had been here at least two growing seasons to have collected so much. He wondered how no one at the castle had known she was here.

David sat up tensely at a sudden thought. *What did one person need with so much?* Perhaps there were others! A band of thieves or gypsies. "When will your husband return?" David asked, carefully probing for information.

"My husband?" Odethia questioned in return, then laughed. "I have no husband. I live here alone."

"But aren't you afraid of bandits out here in the forest?" David inquired, surprised at her blunt reply.

"What would they steal from me?" she said, her hands sweeping the room's contents. "My herbs?"

"You are a healer then?"

"A healer? I guess you could say that. I have come in search of a healing for myself and a new order for the place I left behind."

"My mother knew much about herbal remedies. Are you suffering from an illness?" David asked worriedly.

"Some think so," she said, smiling. "But don't worry. It is nothing you can catch, unless you or I wish it so."

David found her answers confusing, and he felt far from comfortable in her presence. *Where had she come from? What was she doing here?* He must gain more information from her. Perhaps the tea would help him think more clearly.

At that moment, Odethia seemed to appear before him with a cup of tea and a biscuit. *Why hadn't he noticed her approach?* He really must pay more attention to what he was doing. He took the plate and cup from her and sipped the hot liquid. It was slightly sweet and fruity, but with a strange, bitter aftertaste. He felt it all the way down his throat, so warm and soothing. David glanced up at Odethia, who was seated across from him with her own cup in hand. "What is this?" he asked.

"My own special blend," she replied softly. "Do you like it?"

David took another swallow. "I think so," he said, absentmindedly taking a bite of the biscuit. He looked into her eyes. They drew him in and held him captive like the caged bird.

"Then drink it all," cooed Odethia with a small smile.

David felt compelled to put the cup to his lips and drink again deeply. As he did, all fear was swept away. He felt warm and relaxed. He felt as though he had come home after being away for so long, and that was true, wasn't it?

And it suddenly seemed to him that Odethia was his dearest friend. He wanted to tell her about his family, the kingdom, his adventure with Krystin and Mr. Weasel, the defeat of the evil wizard, Zarcon, and everything that had ever happened to him.

And so he did.

CHAPTER 5

David awoke slowly, swimming through the depth of distorted dreams to reach the light at the surface of wakefulness. He felt stiff. His mouth was dry and bitter tasting. He rubbed his eyes trying to clear his vision. *Where was he?* Sunlight shone weakly through a small diamond-shaped window in the low, slanted ceiling. He lay in a small bed. An identical one was nearby. It was so familiar.

"Krystin?" he muttered. He sat up and swung his feet to the floor. The room spun as he cradled his dizzy head in his hands.

When the spinning feeling finally slowed and then stopped, he slowly raised his head and looked around again. *"Of course!"* He was in the cottage loft, his childhood bedroom. *But how did he get here?* He had no memory of what had happened since he rode up to the cottage. *Was that yesterday? Or was it still the same day?*

He stood up and staggered a couple of steps, bracing himself with his hands on the low ceiling. *What had happened to him?*

He heard footsteps below, then tramping up the steep steps up to the loft. A girl with fire-red hair poked her head up through the opening in the floor. She smiled up at him. She looked familiar. *Did he know her?*

"Ah, I see my patient is awake! How are you feeling this morning?

"I'm a bit unsteady," David replied weakly.

"Well, that's to be expected after such a fall," she said sympathetically, as she completed her climb into the loft. "You'd better sit back down."

"A fall?" David exclaimed. "When did I fall?"

"Why, yesterday," the girl explained innocently. "I found you unconscious next to your horse and brought you here."

"I fell off my horse?" David said surprised, as he stumbled back onto the bed. "I don't remember that!" He had taken to riding well and had never been unseated before.

"Don't worry. It's quite common to lose some memory after a fall," the girl replied. "I'm Odethia."

"My name is David, and I guess I owe you thanks."

"Not at all!" Odethia said, smiling. "Some say I have a magic touch when it comes to fixing things. And when you're made better, you can help me out with a few little things."

"I'd be happy to," said David, rubbing his aching head.

"I'm sure you will," Odethia stated, smiling again, though there was a hard edge to her words. "Does your head hurt?" she went on sweetly.

"Yes, as a matter of fact. It's really pounding, and I feel dizzy"

"You may have hurt yourself more seriously than I thought," the girl replied. She fixed her eyes on David's and he suddenly felt weak. "You just lie back and I'll bring you a nice drink to help you become stronger." He lay down as ordered and closed his eyes. Perhaps a drink would help him feel better.

In a few minutes, Odethia came up with the cup and handed it to David as he heaved his unwilling torso up on his elbow and groaned. He looked at the liquid. It was deep green and smelled horrid. He looked up at Odethia and made a sour face.

"Well," she said, "you can't expect medicine to be as sweet as honey, can you?"

"I guess not," David replied quietly. He moved to put the cup down, but Odethia stepped up to him quickly and took his hand. Her warm touch made him look up into her face and eyes, those green eyes! The pain in his head increased.

"David," Odethia said quietly, but firmly, "you must drink this. It will make you strong and powerful."

David tried to think, to pull back away from her gaze. "But I don't . . . ," he began weakly.

"Drink!" she ordered, tipping the cup to his lips.

He gulped it down, then shuddered and choked. Some of it trickled down his chin. It wasn't hot but it burned his skin. He wiped his face on his sleeve. "What <u>was</u> that?" he choked. But that was all he could manage to say. A wave of dizziness washed over him and he fell back, curling into a ball on the bed. Then the blackness of drugged unconsciousness took him completely.

David awoke in the dark of night. *How long had he been here?* He had lost track of time. His head pounded in time with his heartbeat and he felt groggy. Something was happening to him. Something inside. He was sweating and feverish. His throat was dry. *Was it his imagination or was the bed he laid on getting smaller than the last time he awoke? When was that?* His shoulders were broader than the bed was wide and he could no longer fully extend his legs without them slipping off the end. His back ached. His head ached. His skin felt rough, almost scaly. He closed his eyes and was haunted by an intense vision of glowing, green eyes. *Odethia! What was she doing to him?* He had to get up. He had to get out.

He fought to calm the thudding behind his eyes so he could focus in the darkness. Sitting up only intensified the hammering in his skull. He stood and nearly cried out from the pain. Something was wrong with his body. It felt awkward and heavy. He stumbled and cursed his clumsiness. He must be quiet! He took a step. Then another. If he could only manage to get to the ladder steps and out into the cool night air, perhaps his head would clear. He remembered a horse. He had to find his horse and get away. His father might be looking for him by now. *Had it been a week? Or only a few days?*

Inching forward in the darkness, David found the ladder-like steps down from the loft. He turned to back down on hands and knees to steady himself. There was a sudden crashing behind him and a stab of pain as some part of his body hit something in the room. *Oh, no!*

He had to hurry now. The noise would surely awaken Odethia. He reached the bottom of the steps and staggered toward the front door nearly retching with dizziness. He wanted to run, to get away.

Instead he was frozen with shock as he caught a glimpse of his dim reflection in the looking glass on the wall. His hands flew to his face and he screamed in horror.

CHAPTER 6

Odethia advanced into the room, her hair like living flame around her face and eyes glowing like a cat's. Her hands were raised in front of her, pointing at David's back, and her mouth muttering an incantation. "RYMORTO!" she cried.

Before David could take another step, he felt his muscles stiffen like hardening mortar. He fought with all the strength he had to run, to escape from Odethia's advance, but his body was immoveable. Odethia circled around him until she faced him. His eyes, still wide with horror, were the only things he could move. His breathing was shallow gasps.

"So, my young prince," Odethia sneered, smiling wickedly. "You have finally roused yourself to wakefulness. I must have underestimated your strength. But you aren't going anywhere until I am finished with you." She noticed his eyes return to the mirror, and she laughed. "Oh, I'm sorry! You weren't supposed to see your <u>new</u> self until I was finished," she said disappointedly. "I was looking for someone when I came to this world," she began to explain softly. "A wizard by the name of Zarcon! My master! My teacher!" Her voice rose to near screaming, then quieted again. "I came here to find and help him return to our world."

David's eyes narrowed. *Zarcon! She was in league with the wizard!*

"And then <u>you</u> came to call so conveniently and were so weak and <u>willing</u> . . . ," Odethia stopped to laugh again, ". . . to tell me everything I wanted to know and all about how you and your horrible brother and sister led the Great Zarcon to his death!" She stamped the floor, her fists clenched in anger. "And so you will pay!" she screamed in David's face. "And your brother and sister will pay! And your kingdom will pay for his death!"

Odethia looked away from him as she continued loudly. "This magicless world will be so easy to conquer. Then I will make my own world pay as well for driving my master to this wretched place!" She was shaking with rage, but her voice changed. It was quiet, but cold and sharp as an icicle. "And you, my young prince, will help me avenge Zarcon. You will be my means of revenge!"

Odethia paused in her tirade and drew so close to David that he could feel her breath in his face. She whispered now, as if telling him a secret. "You see, David, I'm turning you into a dragon! Isn't that just delicious?" She put her hand to her mouth and giggled. "Just look at yourself!" She pointed to the mirror. "Your skin is already a lovely green and your back spikes and frontal horns are coming in nicely." She danced around him, looking him over carefully. "And your tail!" she nearly screeched. "Oh, you will be a fine and fearsome dragon! A spectacular serpent!" She stopped and cackled, "A serpent for a sorceress! How poetic!"

She continued to twirl as she clapped her hands together gleefully like a tiny child at a party. Then she whirled to face him again and her face grew dark and hateful. "And you will do exactly as I tell you!" Odethia, the sorceress, fixed her eyes upon the prince intently and he felt a stab of pain in his head. "You will be a bad, little dragon, won't you!"

David felt his own will fading. She had bewitched him completely and now he couldn't seem to break her power over him. His mind was losing its sharpness and he couldn't find anything to grab onto. No thoughts to keep his mind from slipping away to dullness and blind obedience to Odethia's commands. Then he

The Serpent and the Sorceress

saw his sister's face in his mind. *Krystin!* He thought desperately. *Where are you now? I need you!* He was helpless to turn his head away as Odethia's luminous eyes bore into his mind, crushing his resistance.

Odethia grinned. "There, there, my pet," she cooed. "Soon you will be in your full glory. There is only one last spell to complete your transformation. And since you were restless tonight, we might as well finish it now."

Crossing to the sitting room fireplace, she poked at the coals and threw in another log and the room grew lighter. Lighting a piece of tinder, she began to circle the room, lighting candles as she went. Soon the room was ablaze with flickering lights.

She set the tinder on the hearth and moved away from David into the kitchen. The sorceress began rattling through her jars for pinches of this and that. She spoke out loud for David to hear.

"Calcium for sharp, strong teeth, powered lizard for form and speed, bat blood for wings to unfurl, diamond dust for impenetrable scales." Odethia continued on and on, then poured the mixed powers into a cup. She took down a bottle filled with a dark liquid and poured some into the cup. It hissed and smoked as it touched the dry ingredients.

Odethia raised the cup in one hand, and retrieving the tinder, set it ablaze again. She turned back toward David with her face and hair reflecting the color of the flame that danced before her eyes. "And now," she crooned, "the final ingredient! The fire that will form in your belly so that you may breathe out death!"

She plunged the burning end into the cup. It sputtered, then there was a loud 'POOF!' and the liquid was set afire. She carefully carried the flaming cup toward David. Smiling slightly, she held it toward him. "Come, my pet! Drink it while it is still hot!" She looked at him with eyes like glowing green embers.

The sorceress uttered a word and David felt his muscles released from the spell that held him rigid. But she held him captive with her eyes and he had no power to resist. He felt his hands reach for the cup; his mouth open and the flaming liquid sear his lips and throat. The burning raced through him filling his whole body, expanding him, igniting a fire within him.

Thin wisps of smoke escaped his nostrils. His body began to change, grotesquely twisting out of human form. His scorched throat stretched longer, his seared tongue thinned, snaking out of his mouth and splitting at its end. He cried out and writhed with agony. His tiny, green scales grew thick, hard. The budding back spikes erupted into a sharp, bristling ridge, shredding his clothes.

He collapsed to all fours and screamed as his leathery, bat-like wings burst forth just below his shoulders. Two horns telescoped from the knobs on his head, and his eyes, while still blue, had cat-like vertical pupils.

With an elongated, snaking neck and lizard-like head, the dragon stood on all fours, its heavy claws raking the wooden floor. Its thick, whip-like tail still twitched at its end like a nervous cat. Its untried wings lay folded across its back and nearly touched the ceiling. Its forked tongue flicked out, tasting the air. Its keen eyes, under heavy, boney brows, surveyed the room. The serpent loomed over the sorceress, its neck bent low in the confines of the room. It felt so alive and powerful! It could easily kill this puny human before it.

David's mind, his will, and his true self were locked away deep in the dull brain of the beast he had become and the controlling power of the sorceress.

Odethia approached her creation with joy. "How handsome you are, my pet!" she gushed, reaching to stroke its smoothly scaled head. The dragon responded to its master with a deep-throated rumbling.

"You are too great to stay inside now, my pet. The night will not be cold for you. And soon it will be daybreak, and with the light comes the morning of my revenge!" Odethia put a hand under the dragon's chin and led him out into the yard, its huge frame barely squeezing through the straining doorway.

The prince's steed, still tethered to the hedgerow, whinnied and reared at the sight of the dragon. The horse backed away, struggling to pull the reins free. The dragon looked at the horse with hunger and hissed a smoky breath. The terrified steed broke loose and fled into the forest. Odethia commanded the dragon be still. She caressed the dragon's head, looking deep into its eyes, "Sleep now, my sweet serpent! There will soon be much for you to eat and do! Sleep now!" The dragon's eyes blinked at her, and then it circled the yard twice, curling up like a puppy to sleep as the first traces of dawn showed in the eastern sky.

CHAPTER 7

"Y ou let him go where?" Aryanne's voice rose a bit. "Stephon, he's just a boy!"

"I was out hunting at his age."

"And you let him go alone? What were you thinking?"

"I was thinking how much I'd like to go with him," the king responded, smiling at his wife. "He'll be fine! He's probably having the time of his life! You know how hard it's been for him here at the castle."

"Oh, Stephon, I'm worried. He's been gone for days. Can't you send some of the soldiers out to find him?"

"Aryanne . . . dear . . . I'm sure he's fine. He promised to be back within the week. Give him another day or two. We must allow him to grow up and be responsible." Stephon put his arms around the queen to comfort her. "He'll be all right."

Aryanne looked up into her husband's eyes. "I hope you are right. Perhaps I *am* being too protective of him." She laid her head against his chest and sighed. Stephon stroked her hair lovingly. She looked up at him again with moist eyes. "If he's not back in two days, will you send some of the men to look for him? Please?"

The king squeezed her a little. "Very well, My Lady," he said with a twinkle in his eye. "I will do as you command!" Stephon bowed low before her.

The queen playfully cuffed him on the arm. "Sometimes you act no better than a stable boy!" she exclaimed, smiling.

"Sometimes I wish that's all I was," the king replied.

Early the next morning, David's horse trotted over the drawbridge dragging its reins. The queen wailed. The king shouted orders. Twenty soldiers thundered through the meadow at a full gallop. They slowed when they reached the forest edge, and spreading out, they methodically began their ordered search for Prince David.

Krystin spent the next hour trying to convince her parents that she should go and talk to the swamp monster, Glurb, or Mr. Weasel, to see if they knew anything about David's disappearance. But having one child missing was quite enough for the royal couple, and they flatly forbade Krystin to leave the castle.

Krystin, of course, took that as a challenge.

CHAPTER 8

Krystin found it easy to slip away into the town of Dayn that had shouldered itself up closely next to the castle's north side. She had borrowed her maid's brown sack-cloth cloak which she threw over the oldest dress she could find in her wardrobe. Walking with her head down, she moved quickly through the market place amidst the sales pitches of the vendors and the bartering and bickering of the buyers. The smells of dried fruits, early spring greens and baked goods mixed with the glittering lure of beads, fabrics and laces were exciting and Krystin was tempted to stop and look more than once. But she was determined to continue with her own task.

The market ended abruptly at a livestock corral and stable. The smell of horse dung was sharp and pungent. An orange cat sat on the last fencepost licking its paw as if trying to clean the smell off.

The town ambled away in a crooked row of thatched roof houses, newly tilled gardens and crisscrossing lines of wagon wheel ruts. The final distraction was a riot of squawking chickens fleeing before a barking dog, and closely followed by the chickens' cursing owner.

Krystin paused to smile, then turned left down the alley between the stable and the house next door. The alley was not much more than a dirt path which led west behind the stable, past some fenced corrals and on into the forested hills. She glanced behind her quickly to make sure she hadn't been followed, and then scampered up the hill and into the trees.

Turning more southward, Krystin stayed just inside the edge of the forest that surrounded the castle on the west and south. She knew it would take the rest of the day to reach Glurb's swamp. She wished that she could have gotten a horse, but that would have attracted too much attention.

No telling what trouble David had gotten himself into. His sister could imagine quite a few things right away. Krystin was so busy with her own thoughts that she nearly didn't see the man crouching in the trees just ahead of her.

She gasped and stopped short, then quickly backed around a large evergreen tree. With her heart pounding loudly, she hoped her mindless crashing through the underbrush hadn't attracted his attention. After several seconds of berating herself for not being more careful, Krystin peered around the tree.

The man hadn't moved. He was looking intently in the direction of the town and castle, as if studying everything carefully. His appearance was quite foreign looking.

The stranger was unusually clean shaven, his thin lips turned down in a serious frown. His black hair was cropped very short. It stood straight up on top and was closely shaved on the sides. He wore a waist-length, dark green jacket with a high collar unlike the longer tunics worn commonly by men of Lyndell. The long, heavy tan leggings with short leather boots cuffed at the ankle seemed odd considering the style was knee pants and high boots. The only ordinary thing about him was the knife at his belt and the bow and quiver of arrows across his back.

Drawing back behind the tree again and pulling her cloak tightly around her, Krystin began to think. She had seen many ambassadors from other lands, but she had never before seen anyone who looked like this man. Maybe he had something to do with David's disappearance. *Was he a bandit holding David for ransom?* Perhaps he was only one of a large group of cut-throats that was hiding out in the forest.

Krystin began to realize that tramping off by herself to see Glurb or find Mr. Weasel was not such a good idea if there were men like this around. Krystin knew she had to get away from here and alert her father. She had to get back to the safety of the castle. *Why had she been so foolish and stubborn?*

She peeked around the tree again. The man was gone!

With renewed panic, Krystin whirled around and ran straight into the stranger. She sucked in a breath and stumbled back off balance, but he grabbed her arms fiercely.

"Let me go!" Krystin cried as she struggled to get away.

"Hasn't anyone ever told you it's not polite to spy on people?" the man said quietly, gripping her tightly. He smiled, but it was a mocking look.

The princess kicked at him, still squirming. "Hasn't anyone ever told you it's not polite to sneak up on people?" Krystin threw back at him. She tried to jerk away again.

"There, there, my little bird! Don't fly off so soon."

Krystin looked up into his thin face. "Who are you?" she demanded.

His nose was straight but rounded at the end. His eyes were very dark brown, in fact almost black under his heavy brows. Krystin was surprised as she realized he was actually very handsome. She felt a blush growing in her cheeks. The man's thin lips twisted up at one corner.

Then, in a matter of seconds, the stranger took Krystin by the wrists and, twirling her around, crossed her arms in front of her, pulling them tight around her, pinning her body against his. The he lifted her feet off the ground forcing her to bend at the waist over her arms, making it impossible for her to get away. Krystin grunted with frustration and pain as she panicked. She had let herself be captured! She was defenseless.

"Maybe I should be asking you the same question," the man retorted. "Who are <u>you</u>, and what can you tell me about this town? Is there a king here?"

"Put me down!" Krystin croaked as the blood rushed to her head. She could barely breathe let alone scream. But she was not going to show her fear to this ruffian. "Why should I answer any of your questions? How do I know you are not some bandit looking to do someone harm. Or maybe you already have!"

"A bandit?" the stranger chuckled. "Is that what you think?"

"And why shouldn't I? You are sneaking around the forest, spying on the town and castle."

"And weren't you doing the same?" the man asked Krystin. "Are <u>you</u> a bandit?"

"Certainly not!" she replied hotly. "I'm Princess Krystin of Lyndell and I demand you let me go!"

The words were out of Krystin's mouth before she realized what she had done. She wished she could suck those words back into her throat and swallow them, but it was too late.

"Oh, I see!" said the man slowly, still smiling. He spoke quietly, leaning close over her. "A princess! That's just perfect because I'm a prince!" He set Krystin gently back on her feet so she could straighten up, although he did not release her arms.

Krystal breathed heavily. Full of anger and fear, she was sure he was mocking her. "And just what is a prince doing out in the forest spying on someone else's kingdom? I think you must be a common thief." The stranger was holding her closely, her back against his chest. She could feel his warmth and breathing.

"Don't be so sure, Princess! If you <u>are</u> a princess. What are you doing out in the forest alone? Certainly the king wouldn't allow his daughter to wander unprotected in a forest so full of bandits and thieves!"

"Let me go, if <u>you</u> are a prince, and I'll tell you." Krystin's face felt warm. His nearness made her uncomfortable.

"First promise you won't run away or put a knife in my back," the man said.

"You promise to let me go if I tell you?"

"Yes, I'll let you go if you answer my questions."

"Very well, I promise not to run away."

"Or put a knife in my back?"

"Or put a knife in your back." Krystin eyed the knife at his belt. "What about <u>me</u>?" she asked.

He raised his hands innocently, stepping back as he released her. "All right, I'll not harm you. Will you answer my questions?"

"I'll answer your questions, <u>if</u> I don't think it will be harmful to the kingdom." Krystin rubbed her sore arms and frowned at the man.

"Well?" he said when Krystin continued to be silent.

"Well, what? You can't expect me to speak to a total stranger when we haven't been introduced, can you?"

"Very well, <u>Princess</u>," the man sighed, frowning as his dark eyes pierced her. "My name is Merrick. I am the son of High Patriarch Brokt of the Realm of en'Edlia. I have come from far away on a quest." He bowed to Krystin, and then added, "<u>Your Highness</u>!"

Krystin curtsied back, and said, "You already know my name. What questions do you have, <u>Prince</u> Merrick?"

"What are you doing out here?"

"Looking for my brother."

"A prince and a princess wandering the forest?"

"Never mind!"

"All right. What town is this?"

"It is Dayn of the Kingdom of Lyndell."

"Who is king here?"

"King Stephon."

"Does he have a wizard in his employ?"

"No."

"Have you ever heard of the wizard Zarcon?"

Krystin's eyes widened at the mention of Zarcon's name. "Zarcon!" she whispered. She looked fiercely at Merrick. "What do you know of Zarcon?" she spat.

"I know he is evil and must be brought to justice for his crimes. Do you know of him?"

Krystin relaxed a little. At least Merrick seemed to be on the side of good, but she was still unsure. It could be a trick. "I know he has been destroyed," she said flatly.

"Destroyed?"

"Yes. And I think you had better come with me and talk to my father."

CHAPTER 9

The dragon opened its eyes. It shook itself and stretched. Its yet unused wings lay folded across its back, but not for long. The dragon was anxious to test its promised power of flight, but it could not fully open its great leathery expanse in such a small space. Somewhere in the back of its brain it dredged up a memory of an open field, a wide meadow clear of trees. Rumbling in anticipation, the dragon trotted off like an excited puppy just as Odethia stepped out of the cottage.

"STOP!" she commanded. The dragon felt her green eyes in its mind and winced. The great lizard stopped and bent its neck toward the sorceress.

"Now where are you going, my pet?" she asked her creation.

Its dim mind was easily confused and it shrugged its massive shoulders, which moved its wings slightly. Then it remembered. It wanted to fly! The dragon tried to extent its wings excitedly and painfully rammed one into a tree. It roared angrily and whirled on the tree as if the tree had attacked it. The beast's anger ignited the fire within and it breathed out a flame that licked the tree, singeing it.

"Wonderful, my pet!" Odethia cried delightedly. "Now come to me," she ordered. The dragon turned and lumbered a few steps closer to the sorceress, lowering its head to see her more clearly. She scratched under its chin and stroked its nose as she peered deeply into its blue eyes.

"And now, my pet, you will do my bidding. You will carry out my revenge for Zarcon's death. You will go to the castle and destroy whatever you can with your fire and claws and teeth. Remember! You hate the castle! It took away your freedom once and now you want to destroy it. The people there don't care for you like I do," she cooed lovingly, stroking its nose. "Beware the soldiers!" she snapped. "They will fear you and try to kill you. But you are strong and brave. Eat whatever you must to fill your belly and fuel your flames. When you tire, return to me."

Odethia's tone returned to gentle quietness as her voice and will filled the beast's mind. "Remember, it is I who love you. It is I who will take care of you." She stroked the great dragon's head.

The dragon felt its fires churning within. It did hate the castle. The castle caused feelings of unhappiness and loneliness. The beast was hungry. It wanted to fly. Odethia's voice and will filled his mind. *She does care, doesn't she? I must obey the one who cares.* The dragon became agitated and anxious, its tail thrashing.

"Now go, my pet!" The sorceress ceremoniously released her serpent to its task. "Go!" She smiled wickedly as she shooed the beast away.

Dancing around, the dragon crashed into the forest, eager to find the remembered meadow, eager to fly, eager to eat. The going was agonizingly slow. The trees were close and its body was large and cumbersome, but it lumbered on. If it became distracted for too long, it was driven on by the green eyes ever-present in its mind.

The dragon continued toward its goal through the night and into the next day. Its stamina seemed boundless, being driven on by hunger and desire. Its eyes were sharp and clear in the dark. It snatched up a roosting pheasant, but it was less than a mouthful. The creature seemed to know the way, but couldn't reason why. Instincts had taken over. Instincts and the sorceress' forces at work within it.

Suddenly, its nose caught a new smell. The great lizard slowed and sniffed, its tongue flickering out to help identify the smell. The scent was horse flesh. The dragon's empty belly rumbled. There was something else. The dragon smelled metal and men. *Soldiers!* They would try to kill what they feared! And they would certainly fear a great dragon. Now its ears heard them advancing noisily through the trees and brush. They were calling out something. *A name?*

"David! Prince David!" the soldiers called as they came. The name sounded familiar to the beast and seemed part of it somewhere deep inside. It tried to find that familiar name, but focus on such tiny things was difficult. Larger things forced their way to the front of its primitive mind. HUNGER. DANGER. ANGER. These it must deal with now.

Commander Ruxton had sent out scouts as was customary. They were to ride ahead and then report back anything noteworthy. So far it had been a quiet ride and his mission was as yet unfulfilled. That suited him fine. He'd rather be out where there was the possibility of action, even battle, rather than cooped up inside the castle walls. He was a large man. Everything about him was large, even his nose. He had huge hands and feet, an expansive chest and broad shoulders. He was half a head or more taller than any man in the king's army and could best any of them in hand to hand combat. With graying hair, he was a seasoned veteran, hardened by long years of war and short rations of food and sleep. He enjoyed a good, long march with his men. When they complained of harsh conditions, Ruxton loved it all the more. He was glad to be in the service of King Stephon again.

The foot soldiers called out as they went, looking through the dense underbrush and in every depression under any rock large enough to conceal a human body. The soldiers on horseback followed, bows and swords within easy reach. Of course they hoped to find the young prince alive, but the commander knew better than to rule out other possibilities.

Ruxton's sharp eyes picked up the distant movement of horse and rider racing toward them through the trees. The commander kicked his mount forward to intercept the returning scout.

"Commander, Sir!" the scout choked out with a stiff salute.

"Well then?" Ruxton returned the salute. "Out with it, Hadley!"

"Sir, there's a . . ." the scout swallowed and stuttered, "there's a . . . a huge beast heading this way. I've never seen anything like it, Sir." The scout looked pale and sweaty. He struggled to control his voice and spooked horse.

"How far?" questioned Ruxton.

"Not more than a few minutes, straight ahead, there," said the scout, pointing.

"Well I've never met a beast I couldn't kill single-handed, Soldier, so with all these men, it shouldn't be a problem, should it?"

"If you say so, Sir," muttered Hadley.

"What was that, Soldier?" Commander Ruxton narrowed his eyes at the scout. Hadley stood high in his stirrups and snapped off another salute.

"Yes, Sir! I mean, no, Sir!"

"All right then. Tell the sergeant to rally the men and form up the ranks. We'll meet this beast head on and eat fresh meat tonight!"

"Yes, Sir!" The scout wheeled his horse away and found the sergeant among those on horseback. The sergeant began shouting at the other soldiers as he trotted around the gathering men. The sound of swords leaving their sheaths rang through the trees.

The dragon finally caught sight of the soldiers. They had swords drawn and arrows notched. Armor covered their heads and chests. Some were mounted on horses. Some were on foot.

DANGER. HUNGER. ANGER. These erupted in the dragon's belly and mind. Its inner fires churned. Roaring with all its might, it charged forward. Rising onto its hind legs, it raked the air with its front claws.

The advancing soldiers came to a shocked, silent halt at the sight of the giant winged lizard. Their mouths gaped open and some began to back away nervously.

"Stand your ground!" ordered the commander. Ruxton was impressed by the shear size of this creature, but quickly snapped into his role as leader. "Archers fire!"

A volley of arrows rained down upon the beast, but the dragon had dropped down on all fours so the shafts thudded dully on its thick scaly neck and shoulders and fell harmlessly to the ground. The beast snapped angrily at the attackers as a thin stream of smoke escaped each nostril.

"Swordsmen charge!" called Ruxton, undaunted. The soldiers hesitated only a moment, then, being trained to face death, they ran at the beast, brandishing their weapons and yelling to keep up their courage.

The dragon continued to advance, roaring as it came. As the first line of swordsmen neared, the serpent's inner fire boiled over and spewed from its mouth, setting brush afire and scorching trees black.

"Shields up!" thundered Ruxton. "Attack!"

The swordsmen inched forward, crouching behind their shields, as the dragon sprayed his fiery breath upon them. One soldier caught fire. His companions leaped to his aid, rolling him on the ground and quickly smothered the flames. They drug him away to safety.

Their shields were no protection as the metal was superheated by the dragon's fire. The men began crying out and dropping their supposed protection, their hands and arms burned. None could get close enough to even strike a blow against this creature.

"Find cover!" shouted Commander Ruxton finally realizing this was no ordinary beast they were dealing with. The soldiers scattered as they struggled to control the frightened horses and haul away the injured. Two men were thrown as their wild-eyed mounts reared and bolted away.

Ruxton knew when to press his men on and when he was outnumbered. He hated losing men without a chance of victory. He could see no way to conquer this formidable monster, at least not with the weapons they had.

"Fall back to the castle!" yelled the commander. Ruxton was brave, but he wasn't foolish.

The mounted soldiers quickly gathered the injured and carried them away. Those who were left ran for their lives or dived into hiding places behind rocks or trees. The galloping horses were able to outdistance the dragon crashing through the underbrush, but not by much.

CHAPTER 10

Krystin and Merrick argued all the way back to the castle. "So you're not a thief, you're a bounty hunter," Krystin reasoned.

"I told you I'm a prince, and while I believe you must work at the castle, you certainly can <u>not</u> be a princess! They have much better manners."

"Well!" huffed Krystin, "We shall soon see about that! And what prince ever got sent out alone on a quest? Where are the rest of your men?"

"And what princess was ever allowed to search the forest alone for her brother?"

"You are an impossible ruffian!"

"Self-righteous scullery maid!"

"Brute!"

"Wench!"

At the portcullis, a guard stopped the bickering pair. "State your business here!"

Already angered by Merrick's bantering, Krystin glared at the guard and threw back her cloak's hood. "I'd be more careful who you let in and out of the castle these days, Doland! What with the prince missing, there could be bandits about."

The guard's eyes went wide as if he had just been awakened from a nightmare.

"Oh . . . oh, <u>Princess</u>! What are you doing outside the castle? Your father strictly ordered that you were not to be given leave. How did you . . . ?" He looked confused and flustered as he glanced around nervously.

"Never mind," Krystin stated in a low voice. "If you don't mention it to the king, I won't mention your lack of attention while on duty! I'm bringing this man to speak with the king."

"Yes, Your Highness!" The guard snapped to attention and saluted. "Thank you, Your Highness!"

"Carry on, Doland!" Krystin waved over her shoulder as she sauntered into the courtyard. She turned to gloat at a surprised Merrick. "See? I <u>am</u> a princess, so there!" Merrick glanced at the guard and shrugged. The guard shrugged back, looking forlorn.

They were silent the rest of the way into the castle as Krystin took Merrick in a side door and then left him in the care of another guard.

"Take him to the doors of the throne room and wait for me there," the princess ordered. "And do <u>not</u> let this man out of your sight!" She ran to hurriedly wash and change her dress before making an appearance in front of her father.

Merrick sighed as he was marched off by the guard.

The king was seated on the raised throne and just finishing kingdom business when Krystin brought Merrick into the throne room for an audience. All heads turned to observe the foreigner at the princess' side and a buzzing of whispers began.

Willier bustled up to Krystin. He was looking wide-eyed and anxious. "Princess!" he whispered when he had drawn near. "It is most unusual for a young woman to accompany a stranger into the presence of the king!"

Krystin looked at Willier, *dear, sweet Willier,* and smiled her sweetest smile, trying to look innocent. "I know, Sir Willier, forgive me, but this man has important information that may help us find my brother." She knew this was stretching the truth a bit, but wanted to make sure Merrick gained the attention of her father without delay.

Willier looked startled and glanced at Merrick, then back at Krystin. "Very well, I shall inform His Majesty." He turned on his heel and hurried to the king's side, who was discussing a property boundary issue with a local dignitary.

Willier bent and whispered in the king's ear. The king looked up in Krystin's direction and nodded. Quickly excusing himself, he left the throne room for his private chambers.

Willier announced an hour recess in court business and dutifully overturned the sand-filled hourglass on the bailiff's table. There was murmuring in the crowd as they began to shuffle out. Willier then escorted Krystin and her companion to the king's chambers.

"So, Krystin, what have you done now?" her father demanded after Willier had closed the doors.

"Father, I . . ."

"Well? Who is this and what information does he have?" King Stephon asked impatiently.

Merrick stepped forward and bowed. "If you will permit me, Your Highness, King Stephon, I will explain."

The king looked severely at Merrick. His trained eye took in every detail. "So you are a well-bred young man, perhaps even high-born. And not from anywhere remotely close. Do you know anything about the disappearance of my son, David?"

"Your Majesty, I am indeed a prince in a far off realm. I have journeyed here to fulfill a quest. Sadly, I know nothing of your son. I have come in search of the wizard Zarcon. He is an evil renegade and has committed many crimes and must be brought to justice."

"Your quest comes too late, for Zarcon is dead. But he did indeed cause my family much grief, in fact years of sorrow and suffering before his demise."

"I would like to hear your story, if you are willing to share it with me. That way I can have evidence to present to my father when I return."

"Yes, but first I would like to know by what road you came to our kingdom. Did you see anything of a 14-year-old boy in your travels? My son's horse returned from the forest to the southwest without him, and I fear he may have fallen into the hands of bandits." The king turned and walked toward the council table.

"I did come through a part of the forest, but from the north. I met . . . ." Merrick paused as he glanced at Krystin. She pleaded with her eyes. "I met no one," he continued.

Krystin smiled and lowered her eyes. *He hadn't given her away!* She knew now that she could trust him.

The king leaned against the table and lowered himself into a chair with a sigh. "I was hoping you had news. My wife is quite distraught over our son. But that is not your business now. I will tell you what I know of Zarcon, and then you may return to your own realm." He motioned for Merrick to sit with him. "Krystin, you may as well stay and add what you know," he said wearily.

Merrick and Krystin seated themselves as the king launched into the tale of how Zarcon had come to Lyndell and all that had happened previously because of his wickedness.

The search party of soldiers kicked their lathered horses to full speed when they reached the open meadow. They shouted out warnings as they came. The confused group of soldiers at the drawbridge and on the wall battlements strained to hear, but were not able to make out the words being yelled to them.

As the dragon crashed through the last of the trees and into the meadow, words were no longer needed. Everyone scrambled behind the stone walls and waited nervously for the fleeing soldiers to clear the portcullis so it could be dropped, the gates could be shut and the drawbridge pulled up.

The alarm spread rapidly through the castle.

CHAPTER 11

There was an insistent banging on the king's chamber doors and a muffled voice yelling, "Your Highness! King Stephon! Come quickly! We're under attack!"

Yelling orders as he went, the king, with Willier, Krystin and Merrick trailing behind, was soon on the castle wall overlooking the southwest meadow. The battlements were lined with bowmen while officers rallied other soldiers below for a ground assault if needed.

The royal party stared out at the terrifying beast below who had captured a horse in its huge hind claws and was devouring it. "What in the name of heaven is it?" cried the king turning on Willier.

"I have never seen anything like it, Your Highness." Willier shrugged, looking baffled and quite terrified.

"It's a dragon," Merrick stated calmly.

"Where did it come from?" Stephon questioned Merrick. "Do we have need to fear it?"

"Yes, it can be very destructive to humans and animals alike. This appears to be a young one, but it can fly and most likely breathe out fire as well."

"Breathe out fire? What sort of magic is this? Does the fire not consume the beast?"

"It is part of its nature," Merrick continued to explain. "It has an inner source of flame that it can spew forth at will without harming itself."

"But where did it come from?" the king asked again.

Prince Merrick thought a moment, and then replied slowly, "If dragons are not natural to your world, then it has either come from my world or has been created magically. I find it hard to believe that this dragon could have found the portal accidentally. Are you sure there are no wizards or sorceresses in the area?"

"What are you talking about? My world? Your world? The portal?" King Stephon squinted at Merrick. "I think there must be more you need to tell me, young prince!"

Merrick opened his mouth to speak, but at that moment the dragon stretched its wings and flapped them experimentally. It raised its head and roared for joy as it lifted off the ground leaving the remains of its meal behind.

The dragon's belly was full and the soldiers were gone. *No more hunger. No more danger.* Green eyes burned in its brain. *Anger. Anger. ANGER!* It looked down at the castle. *Yes, anger!* It hated the castle. It must destroy the castle. It flapped higher and higher, gaining altitude.

"What is it doing now?" asked Willier innocently, watching the dragon ascend.

At that moment, as they all stared up at the strange creature in the sky, it folded its wings in a dive straight at the castle.

"Get down! It's attacking!" yelled Merrick. Everyone ducked low as the dragon raked the parapets with its claws, bellowing savagely.

"Your Majesty!" Willier was tugging on Stephon's robe, urging him away from the open walls. "It is not safe for you here! Let the soldiers deal with this beast!"

With the dragon's next pass, it breathed out fire just skimming over the place where the king and his company huddled. They felt the searing heat ripple over them. One soldier screamed and tumbled off the wall in a ball of flames, landing in the moat, while several others were blackened and scorched.

At that moment Commander Ruxton appeared. "At your service, Your Highness!" he bowed hastily.

"I'll have your report when this situation is under control, Commander," stated the king quickly. "Take over here," Stephon ordered, turning the battle over to Ruxton's expertise. "I'll be below. Send regular reports on the situation."

Ruxton snapped off a salute. "Yes, Your Highness!" The commander turned and ran toward his men. "Take cover!" yelled Ruxton to his soldiers. "Fire at will!"

With those commands, the royal party retreated into the safety of a tower. Stephon rounded on Merrick again. "How can we defeat this beast?"

"Your Highness, were we in my world I would know exactly, but here I am unsure. I must learn more about the dragon. I must find out if it is natural or magically crafted."

"Do what you must, but do it quickly!" demanded the king. "And we will talk more of your world later!"

"Yes, Your Highness!" Merrick bowed then turned and ran up the tower stairs. Stephon descended the spiral staircase with Willier at his heels.

Merrick had to get closer in order to be able to see into the dragon's mind and feel what powers were at work there. He ran on as he heard the serpent pass again and a volley of arrows clinking harmlessly on its scales. It roared and soared upward again while Merrick scaled the stairs two at a time, racing to get to the open tower.

As Merrick surged upward, he began to hear another set of footsteps echoing his own. He might have wondered if the king had sent a soldier up with him had he not noticed the distinct swishing sound of a long dress also. He knew it was Krystin.

He really didn't want anyone with him. He didn't want to reveal his powers. His father had given him strict instructions not to do anything to attract undue attention. But now he could see this was going to be difficult in light of the sudden appearance of the dragon, a magical beast in this mundane world. *Strange*, he thought.

Merrick rounded the last few steps breathing heavily. He looked around for a window or door out onto the turret. He found a door that led out to a narrow walkway. Scanning the sky, he located the dragon's form just making a high turn heading for another pass at the castle. He might have time to reach into the dragon's mind before it swooped by him.

Concentrating on the dragon, Merrick looked steadily at it, drawing himself closer mentally, reaching out with his mind. He felt the touch of the dragon's raw, instinctive feelings. *Anger. Danger.* Merrick probed deeper. He began to see bits of memory. These were not the remembrances of a natural dragon! There were traces of family, home, a childhood! The dragon was an enchanted human! Who could have done this, but Zarcon?

Merrick pushed a bit deeper, trying to find a trace of the master of this beast. He heard the dragon roar as it was nearly upon him. Just a moment longer! Merrick squinted his eyes, and invoked a magical charm to aid him, and suddenly he was met with resistance.

An image of glowing green eyes sent a searing glance into his mind. Merrick withdrew in pain and broke the contact. The dragon suddenly banked toward the tower where Merrick stood, roaring and licking the air with its forked tongue as it came. The prince quickly rolled through the doorway and nearly collided with Krystin as the dragon breathed out flames and set the conical roof on fire just above their heads.

Merrick leaped to his feet and hauled Krystin back down the steps while flames licked their heels and blackened the walls and stairs above them. The two continued their descent as the dragon continued to rake the turret with tooth and claw as its wings fanned the flames.

Then suddenly, for no apparent reason, the dragon broke off its vicious attack, and flew away, straight over the trees at the meadow's edge and out of sight.

CHAPTER 12

After spending a great deal of time comforting his frightened citizens and sending out a proclamation on the issue of the dragon, King Stephon heard Commander Ruxton's report and then ordered Krystin and Merrick join him again in his council chambers.

"Now, my young prince," the king demanded, "you will tell me what you are all about! What is this talk of <u>your</u> world and <u>my</u> world? What did you find out about the dragon? How did you send it away? Are you a wizard then? What are your intentions here?"

Merrick sighed and looked uncomfortable. He began to wish he had the power to disappear, but that was a weakness in him. "Very well, Your Highness, I will tell you what you want to know. But I need your word that it will not leave this room. You must appreciate that I am sworn to protect my own realm and people's safety."

The king glanced around the room, and then quickly dismissed the guards and Willier, who protested all the way out the door. The door had not completely closed when it opened again showing Krystin's anxious face. "Not right now, Krystin," her father stated hotly. But as she slowly began to withdraw, Merrick spoke up.

"Actually, Your Highness, with your permission, I'd like the princess to hear what I have to say."

The king looked quizzically at Merrick, who continued, "She has had much experience with Zarcon's wizardry and may be helpful in solving the mystery of the dragon."

"Very well," conceded Stephon. "Come in and sit down, Krystin."

Krystin's faced reddened slightly, but she was delighted to be included. She quickly closed the door and took her place at the table, riveting her attention on Merrick's handsome face.

The prince sighed again and looked down at his hands clasped in front of him on the glossy table top. "Where shall I begin?" he said mostly to himself. His face grew serious, his dark eyes focused on nothing in the room as he began his tale. "I am Merrick, son of High Patriarch Brokt and High Matriarch Narrian, and heir to the throne in the Realm of en'Edlia on the world of Irth."

"Earth? That is <u>our</u> world!" broke in Stephon.

"Ironically, our worlds have names that sound the same, yet they are so different. My Irth is spelled I-R-T-H, Your Highness. Ours is a world where all people are born with at least one magical gift which requires training to focus and control it. We are not workers of evil, but peaceable people."

He paused, looking straight at Stephon, allowing his words time to be digested. When the king remained quiet, Merrick continued.

"Many, many years ago there was a man named Zarcon in en'Edlia who grew dissatisfied with how the government was being run by my father. He began to gather others to him in order to overthrow the realm and claim it as his own. He was a powerful wizard and did much damage, corrupting others with his beliefs, before he was defeated."

"We understand that well here in Lyndell also," said the king sadly.

Merrick went on, "He was banished to one of our outer moons as punishment. However before we could confine him there, he somehow escaped. He disappeared and we have searched for him ever since."

Intrigued, Stephon questioned, "How is it possible to travel between worlds as you do?"

"We have portals, doorways if you will, that allow travel between our world and others. The inherent magic of our world makes this possible. It is part of every living thing there. When Zarcon escaped, we could only assume he fled by way of these portals to another world. It is only now that we have come to your world to continue our search and bring Zarcon back to live out his exile for his crimes. This is the first place that I have been able to find any trace of him. You say he was destroyed, yet now there is a dragon here. Is it possible you are mistaken?"

Krystin spoke up. "I saw him eaten alive by Glurb, the guardian of the swamp and forest." Krystin shivered as she remembered Glurb's battle with Zarcon. "Some would call Glurb a monster, but he was a hero and friend to me."

"I did not witness that," put in the king, "but the children said that Zarcon's spells over them were broken after that. It seems that would indicate the end of his power."

"So it would seem," replied Merrick, thinking.

"And what of the dragon?" Stephon spoke up loudly, gesturing with his hands. "What do you know of it?"

"I know that it is not a dragon by nature." Merrick stated. "It was human, probably some poor peasant, and now, through magic, it is the beast you have seen."

Krystin drew in a shocked breath.

"How do you know this?" demanded the king, his eyes narrowing.

Merrick sighed again. "I have the ability to see within the mind of both animals and humans. It is one of my gifts."

"So do you pry into everyone's mind?" The king was still feeling threatened and uneasy. "Do you search for secrets of my kingdom within my mind?"

"No, Your Highness!" Merrick replied quickly. "I do not <u>pry</u>, as you say, into human minds unbidden. It is against our laws. It is different for animals. Besides, you might have felt my presence in your mind unless you were sleeping, and even then perhaps."

"Very well. Continue. How were you able to send the dragon away?"

"I had nothing to do with that," Merrick said. "I believe that was done by the dragon's creator and master. When I was in the dragon's mind, I felt another presence which detected me and tried to do me harm. I withdrew and the dragon attacked me. Then it just flew away."

"Can you identify this other presence? The one you say is the dragon's creator?" the king questioned relentlessly.

"No, not completely. I did get the impression of glowing, green eyes staring at me and . . ." Merrick paused to reflect. "And those eyes were definitely female. Which means it couldn't be Zarcon, it would have to be a sorceress." He looked at Krystin.

"I'm not a sorceress!" she cried, looking shocked.

"Of course not," her father and Merrick said at the same time.

King Stephon pushed away from the table and got up to pace by the window while pondering these new revelations.

Merrick continued to look at Krystin. His eyes were like black pools that drew her in and looked into her very soul. She could not look away. The entire room seemed to disappear and all she could see were Merrick's eyes. She felt light, as though she might float away any second.

Merrick spoke, his voice rich and low. "You would have to have been born on my world to be a sorceress, but you are rather bewitching just the way you are." The corner of his mouth turned up slightly.

"You <u>are</u> a scoundrel!" Krystin whispered as she felt herself smile and grow very warm.

"Then," her father's voice fractured the moment, "we are dealing with a new threat to the safety of my kingdom and people beyond what the dragon imposes. We must find this sorceress and stop her. If we stop her we will also stop the dragon. Am I right?" Stephon stopped pacing to face them.

Merrick's attention snapped back to the king. "That is correct, Your Highness."

"And very possibly find my son, David, as well." The king leaned on the table. "Perhaps he is her hostage. Zarcon held Eron captive as he worked his evil, perhaps it is the same now." He looked at Merrick seriously. "So how will you do it?" he inquired.

"Do it?" asked Merrick, confused by the question.

"Yes, yes!" snapped the king impatiently. "How will you rid us of this sorceress? Surely you have the power to do so! You did come here to capture Zarcon, did you not? And now here's a sorceress whose power surely can not exceed you own."

Merrick sat back in his chair and stared up at the king. "Uh, well, Your Highness, I, uh, guess we have to find her first."

"Very well," stated the king decisively. "If my soldiers can find her, can you deal with her? Take her back to your world or dispose of her or something?"

"I believe I will have to, Your Highness. It was my quest to bring back Zarcon or news of his demise, but now I feel compelled to find out who this woman is and what she is doing here. Dealing with a sorceress is different than dealing with a wizard, but if she is from my world then she is breaking our laws by using her magic for evil purposes in a non-magical world."

"Good!" Stephon declared. "Then I propose a trade."

"A trade, Your Highness?" Merrick was surprised again by the king's words.

"Yes." King Stephon folded his arm across his chest and grinned slightly. "If you prove your goodwill by ridding us of the dragon and sorceress, or whoever is behind this, I would like to establish a relationship of peace between our worlds. Would your father be open to receiving a foreign minister from Lyndell?"

Merrick smiled and glanced at Krystin. "I believe he would, Your Highness."

The king extended his hand across the table, which Merrick firmly grasped. "Then we have work to do," said Stephon with grim determination.

CHAPTER 13

The next day the castle was humming with preparations being made to send a large group of soldiers with scouts out in search of the dragon and sorceress. The king spent the night interviewing Commander Ruxton and the soldiers who had encountered the dragon in the forest, asking about the direction from which the creature had come and where exactly they were in the forest. He had spread out maps of the area, carefully charting in the locations of the old cottage, the swamp and some of the other prominent features he had noted as they moved back to the castle and that he had found in his years hunting around the cottage.

King Stephon, Ruxton and Willier were now staring at a large circle that was drawn on the map. The cottage was indeed inside that circle as the king had suspected and feared. He hoped his son was alive out there in the forest somewhere. Maybe he was even at the cottage itself.

There was a soft rap on the door as it creaked open. Stephon glanced up to see his wife's face peering at him from around the door. "Stephon? Any news of David?"

The king sighed and looked down at the map. He did not want to answer.

The queen came to his side, glancing down to see what was holding the king's attention. "I heard that a stranger had come with news." She noticed the cottage marked on the map.

Stephon dismissed Willier and Ruxton before he told Aryanne about Merrick, the dragon and the sorceress.

The queen's face grew tense as she listened. "You don't suppose that David is . . ." her voice trailed off, not wanting to speak her fears. The king sighed again and put his hand over the queen's hand.

"Aryanne, we must assume that our son is somewhere out there, perhaps being held against his will by this sorceress." The queen's eyes filled with tears as her husband continued. "We must continue to hope that he is alive and that Merrick can defeat the sorceress once we have found her."

"Oh, Stephon!" Aryanne sobbed. "It's happening again! I can't live through this a second time! First Eron and now David! What shall we do?"

The king embraced her and stroked her hair. "I swear to you, as King of Lyndell, that I will not sit idly by this time! I will use all the power at my command to find and bring our son home!"

"I know you will," the queen whispered in reply.

After a few more moments in his comforting embrace, Aryanne released her husband to return to his work. She fled with her sorrows and fears to the royal bedchambers. The servants built up the fire in her room and draped her with blankets, but she still shivered as she stared into the flames. She never heard the hundreds of tromping feet as the soldiers marched across the drawbridge and into the forest to begin their search with orders to capture or kill, if necessary, either the dragon or the sorceress.

Krystin walked slowly along one of the many long corridors deep inside the castle, her arms wrapped about herself as she thought about all that had happened. *What would her father do now? How would Merrick defeat the sorceress? How could a person*

be turned into such a terrible beast? Would the soldiers or Merrick have to kill the dragon? Where was David?

She thought about all that had happened in her encounter with Zarcon that seemed so long ago yesterday, but now seemed too close. She shivered at the memory of his wickedly smiling face.

"Does the princess needs a cloak?" asked a voice so close that Krystin jumped and cried out. She turned to see Merrick's sparkling eyes and grin, upturned at one corner of his mouth.

"Stop sneaking up on me!" Krystin cried with irritation. "Your Highness!"

Merrick bowed low before her, and then seemed to pull a long blue cloak out of the air, which he draped around her shoulders.

"How did you . . . where . . ." she sputtered with amazement.

"I was not sneaking! It is not my fault if you are dull of hearing," remarked the prince, still grinning as he stepped back.

Krystin turned in a huff and continued walking and Merrick fell into stride beside her. "Perhaps my eyes are also not as sharp as they should be!" she said glancing over at the prince and pulling the cloak tighter around her.

They walked on a ways then Krystin sighed.

"I'm sorry, Prince Merrick. I guess I was just lost in thought. Thank you for the cloak." She offered a smile to Merrick who nodded a bow.

"Please just call me Merrick. We need not be so formal in private conversations."

"I'm so worried about my brother," Krystin continued. "We've been through so much together. I hate just waiting around. I want to go out there and find him."

"I know what you mean," replied Merrick seriously. "I have two younger brothers myself, and a little sister. Besides, you already tried your own rescue mission, remember?"

Krystin scowled at him. "I might have found him if I hadn't run into you."

"Tell me about your brother," the prince said, sounding sincerely interested.

Krystin took several more steps before saying anything.

"I was about two and a half when he was born. We grew up in a small cottage in the forest, as you have heard," Krystin began slowly. She talked on about their life there and how happy they had been. About David's hunting trips with their father, games they played to pass the time and the loft they had shared at night. She smiled as she spoke. Those had been happy, carefree times.

Merrick remained silent, listening.

"And in our loft there was this wonderful little window in the roof that let in the moonlight by night and sun by day," Krystin was saying.

Suddenly Merrick stopped. Krystin took a few steps before she noticed. She paused and looked back. "What's the matter?" Merrick stood still, his eyes were seeing something far away. Krystin walked back to him. "Are you all right?" she asked, touching his arm.

Merrick looked at her finally and asked, "Did your brother ever catch a rabbit?"

Krystin looked at Merrick, puzzled by his odd question. "Yes, of course," she replied. "He and Father were always bringing home game. Now that you mention it, I think the first thing he ever trapped was a rabbit. He was so excited! I just wanted him to let it go."

Krystin chuckled at the memory. But the prince was not smiling; in fact his face was so serious it alarmed her.

"Krystin," he said, "I think I'd better tell you what I saw in the dragon's mind."

Now it was Krystin's turn to listen in silence as Merrick poured out to her everything he had dimly seen and felt as he had entered the mind of the dragon.

He told her of the poor looking family of mother, father, and sister. He told her of a happy feeling of triumph at the first rabbit snared as a proud father looked on. He told her of diamond-shaped glass with moonlight shining through. He told her of a damp, darkness filled with voices and an angry feeling connected to the castle and a strong desire to be free. He told her of a little song about moonbeams and starlight that floated in and out. He told her of a small glowing object in someone's hand. He told her of a joyful feeling relating to finding a brother.

All those memories were in the dragon's mind. All those memories that sounded so familiar to Krystin. She felt confused and suddenly frightened.

"What does it mean?" asked Krystin, alarmed. She could feel goose bumps prickling her arms. "What are you saying?"

"I'm trying to tell you," Merrick said slowly, taking her arms gently in his hands, "that I think your brother, David, is the dragon."

"NO!" Krystin shouted and pulled away. "No, it can't be!" She drew back from Merrick, horrified at the thought. "Those could be anyone's memories! Anybody could have done those things."

She squeezed her eyes shut and pressed her clenched hands to them. She did not want to believe it, but in her heart she knew Merrick was right. "No," she whispered between ragged breaths as tears made tracks on her checks. "Oh, no. Oh, David!"

Merrick put a comforting arm around her. "Krystin," he said softly. "We must tell your father."

Krystin's head snapped up, her eyes wide. "Father! The soldiers!" She looked at Merrick frantically. "They're going to kill David!"

CHAPTER 14

Merrick wished he had the power to teleport himself from place to place like his cousin, Smich, or fly like his brother, Jarrius. Actually it wasn't flying. It was more like directed levitation, but there were so many times when those talents could come in handy. Now was one of them.

His thoughts urged the horse beneath him on to greater speed. It had taken too long to convince the king that he, Merrick, should be the one to go. He should have gone with the soldiers in the first place, but Stephon had insisted he remain safely behind the castle walls until the sorceress could be more precisely located. The king had not wanted to lose his greatest weapon in a premature mishap.

Now Merrick was playing a desperate game of catch-up. He probed ahead with his mind to find the mass of soldiers. He could feel their anxiety and restlessness, but still a long way off. Their path was easy to follow, but he had to slow his mount once the forest closed in around him. The prince still had not formed an adequate plan to defeat the sorceress. Time for that was short now. He must think. Prodding the horse's mind again with thoughts of urgency, Merrick turned his thoughts inward as he concentrated on possible tactics.

Krystin had assaulted her father with every excuse she could dream up as to why she should be allowed to go with Merrick. She cried and shouted and pled and wept. Her father had finally commanded her to be still and confined her to her room until she could calm down. She had fled to the queen's chambers, but one look at her mother's stricken face, and she felt the queen's deep sadness.

Krystin knew better than to add to her mother's distress, and so gave her a quick hug. "I love you, Mother!" she whispered. Then she retreated to her own room where she screamed and ranted and finally threw herself on the bed and cried. When her anger and frustration was finally exhausted, she sat up and began to think.

Someone in the family had to do something! Mother would be no help at all. Father had sent soldiers to kill the dragon and Merrick to warn them. But what if he failed? And what did Merrick care? <u>He</u> might hurt David if he had to defend himself against the dragon. Or maybe worse! There was no one else. She had to go and help her brother. She had gotten out of the castle unnoticed once before and she could do it again. She needed a horse this time. That would be tricky.

Not long after Merrick's horse had clattered over the drawbridge and out into the meadow and forest beyond, Krystin was slinking away from her room with plans to follow him.

Commander Ruxton was sending men ahead to surround the cottage. He was a man of war, knowledgeable and skilled in military tactics. But he knew nothing of magic. His plan was to verify the sorceress was indeed in the cottage and then to make her his prisoner and take her back to the castle. It was simple and direct. Why waste valuable time sending a messenger back to the castle and then waiting for this Prince Merrick, whoever-he-was, to come and take care of the sorceress. Could one man do more than all his ranks of soldiers? It was out of the question.

Ruxton reasoned that the king had certainly been overly distraught and had not thought this through properly. During the council, the king had barely asked him to give advice on tactical procedures.

So now he would handle things his way and the king would be happy to have it over with so soon. The only problem might be the appearance of the dragon again. But he had enough men this time to divert the beast while the capture was taking place. What had the king said? *Subdue the sorceress and you will subdue the dragon as well.* And that was his plan.

With his men in position around the quiet forest cottage, Ruxton shouted out, "You in the house! Come out and surrender by order of King Stephon! You are surrounded! Come out!"

There were a few tense moments of silence, then the front door of the cottage creaked open just a crack. A timid feminine voice called out, "Who are you? What do you want? Please don't hurt me!"

Stepping forward out of his concealed place, the commander sheathed his sword. "I am Commander Ruxton. We don't want to hurt you, Miss. We have come by order of the king. Are you a sorceress?"

The door opened farther and Odethia stepped out into the light. She looked very frail and harmless. She smiled warmly at the commander as she focused her bright, green eyes upon him. "Do I look like a horrible, old sorceress to <u>you</u>, Commander Ruxton?"

Ruddick felt her eyes draw him in and hold him spellbound. She was indeed young and beautiful. "No, Miss," he mumbled.

The second-in-command stepped up behind Ruxton and said something in his ear. The commander turned away, breaking the contact with Odethia. He shook his head feeling a bit dizzy for a moment. "Yes, yes," he said suddenly, turning back toward Odethia. "My second reminds me that you must come along to see the king no matter what. Will you give me your word to come peacefully?"

Odethia continued to smile as she glanced around the clearing. She could see and feel the presence of many soldiers in among the trees. She would never be able to use her magic to control so many. They would overpower her in no time by sheer brute force. They left her no choice.

"I would love to see the king," the sorceress cooed sweetly. "May I take along my little pet? He may get lonely if I leave him here." Odethia did her best to look innocent.

Commander Ruxton scowled but said, "Very well, get your pet and let's be off." He would be glad when this whole affair was over and he could get back to the important business of protecting the kingdom against real threats instead of escorting harmless women to the castle.

He called to his men to form ranks and mount up and had his second and one other step up to escort the woman and her pet to the extra horse they had brought for just this purpose.

Odethia disappeared into the house only to step back out empty-handed. "Oh, Commander!" she cried out, waving her hand. "Here comes my pet now"!

Ruxton looked back at the woman in confusion. Several horses reared, rolling their eyes. A sound like canvas tents flapping in the wind was heard low over the trees, and then the dragon swooped down and landed heavily right in front of the cottage in the small clearing.

Horses bellowed and bolted, tearing their reins from their riders' hands and crashing through the underbrush. The commander shouted to his men to take cover but hold their ground. Soldiers ducked under cover of bush and tree and rock as the dragon roared and stomped the ground.

From a protected place behind a large tree, Ruxton watched in amazement as the sorceress calmly walked to the side of the dragon and patted its flank lovingly. *Truly she was the key to caging the beast,* he thought.

"I don't think I'll be going with you today, Commander," the sorceress called out to him in a sweet voice. "My pet is a little restless. But do come back and visit us again sometime! Oh, and Commander, you can tell the king that I <u>will</u> be calling on him soon. And I'll be <u>sure</u> to bring my pet along!"

Ruxton was angry now. He didn't like being made a fool of, especially in front of his men. "You <u>will</u> come with us by order of the king!" he shouted from behind a tree. "We will take you by force if necessary!"

"Very well, Commander," Odethia called back. "You are welcome to try!" She turned to the dragon then and said, "I guess they want to play, my pet!"

Her eyes glowed in the dragon's mind. It roared and stomped. ANGER! DANGER! It lifted its wings, and lowering its head, breathing out the fire in its belly.

CHAPTER 15

Krystin had trotted her horse to just inside the edge of the trees. It had taken a bit longer to skirt the meadow, but she had avoided being seen that way.

Being a princess had its advantages. She had lots of coins and jewelry to bribe, bargain and buy what she needed. Wearing breeches and a tunic like a boy, she had tucked her hair up into a hat, and then followed a wagon with an extra horse tied to it out of the castle walls, past the guards and into the town. She was able to buy the horse from the wagon owner and quickly make her way to the place where she had encountered Merrick and beyond, deeper into the forest toward the cottage.

Merrick heard the soldiers before he saw them. The sound of battle echoed through the trees. And above it all the roaring of the dragon. Merrick knew these brave men had no idea what they were dealing with. He had to find Commander Ruxton before they could hurt the dragon. He no longer worried about being heard himself and urged his horse on, crashing through the undergrowth. He came up behind a chaotic scene.

The soldiers had surrounded the dragon and were taking turns lunging at it while others diverted its attention. Commander Ruxton was shouting orders continually, directing the men to thrust forward or fall back. The dragon's thick scales were protecting its back and sides, but occasionally a soldier would prick its more tender underbelly. This would only cause the dragon to rear up and roar, then breathe out a bit of fire.

The sorceress's serpent was confused and tiring from the constant harassment. It was hurting from the arrows that had pierced the thinner membrane of its wings, and bleeding from several small arrow and sword wounds to its belly.

Ruxton had stepped up the attack on the dragon as he saw the beast weakening. He had ordered a few soldiers to go find the sorceress, bind her and bring her back to him. Several other soldiers had been drug away from the fighting, being burned or battered by the dragon.

Merrick leapt off his horse and ran to find the commander. He shouted to him as he approached, but got no response. Finally Merrick reached Ruxton who glanced at him and then returned his attention back to the battle.

"Ah, good man!" he said to Merrick. "You've come to help us defeat the dragon!"

"No, Commander! I've come to tell you not to harm the dragon or the sorceress!" Merrick nearly yelled in his face.

"What? How else shall we defeat this monster? Would you like to ask it to come, pretty please?" Ruxton's face reddened with anger. "We tried that with the woman or sorceress or whatever she is," he shook his fist in Merrick's face. "And this is the result!" His arm swung toward the injured men behind him.

"Commander Ruxton!" Merrick's voice grew quiet and serious. "By order of the King, the dragon is not to be harmed! The dragon is the king's son, David!"

Ruxton raised his eyebrows and looked harshly at the young prince. "You want me to believe that this hideous beast is Prince David?"

"I know you don't understand, but you must believe me! The sorceress has transformed him through her magic and now controls his actions. The king's orders are to capture the sorceress if possible, but not at the risk of injuring either of them."

"It will take more preparations than this if we are to capture this beast," Ruxton threw back at Merrick. "We will need an iron cage and nets and many more men. And what of the woman?"

"Let me see what I can do, Commander."

"You? I've already sent some men to capture the sorceress. I suppose you can help them if you like. Do you want some of my men to come with you?"

"No. See to your men, Commander, and call the others back if you can."

"You'll get yourself killed!" Ruxton called after him.

Merrick slipped away through the trees, ignoring the commander's taunt. He would watch and wait for his time to put his now formulated plan into action. The soldiers might actually prove helpful as a diversion.

Odethia could feel her pet weakening. She could not let it fail! She must find a way to get rid of the soldiers. She sensed the soldiers approaching the kitchen door. She sent her thoughts to the dragon. *Use your fire!* Then turned to deal with these intruders herself.

The dragon saw in its mind what it must do. It lumbered forward, roaring and snapping, causing the soldiers to fall back. Then it breathed out a wall of fire and set the brush ablaze.

Flames leaped up around the trees in front of the soldiers and they were forced to move back. The dragon continued to advance, breathing fire as it went. Soon the cottage was nearly surrounded by a fiery wall.

The fire continued to swell and spread. Ruxton shouted the retreat. He would gladly fight the dragon, but he could not fight the fire.

"Perhaps the fire will be the sorceress's own doom!" he murmured gruffly. "To the castle, men!" he shouted again. "Fall back!"

The commander hung back a few moments looking for the return of the men he had sent to capture the woman. The other soldiers hurriedly picked up their wounded and moved at a run away from the burning brush. If they were lucky the fire would burn itself out before it engulfed them too. Otherwise they would be running for their lives to outdistance the flames.

Ruxton shook his head with a twinge of sad regret that the men did not return. He had hoped to at least capture the sorceress. He was furious at having to return to the castle empty-handed once again, but he could wait for them no longer.

The dragon watched the danger moving away. It licked its smarting wounds. It wanted to eat again, but mostly it wanted to sleep. Odethia's eyes burned in its mind. *Go to the castle! Fly now! Go find food and visit the king! Then you may rest, my pet.*

The dragon's mind curled around a thought of its own. *Danger gone. Hurt. Sleep.*

The sorceress increased the intensity of her command. The dragon roared, writhing with the pain in its head. *GO! NOW! ANGER! HUNGER! GO!*

The dragon reluctantly leaped into the air. Flapping its wings and fanning the flames, it took to the sky, banking toward the castle once more. At least the pain in its head lessened, but its wing was torn and exhaustion threatened to pull it from the sky.

Odethia stepped out to watch her stubborn winged-lizard fly away. She looked out at the spreading fire that licked at the trees and devoured the undergrowth. She had to stop the fire now that the soldiers were gone before it made her homeless and ruined her further plans.

Hurrying inside again, she went to her jars and herbs and quickly mixed together several powders. These she folded into a small, paper packet.

She searched for and found a fallen arrow and tied the packet to it. She smiled as she thought about the retreating soldiers. This would give them a little more incentive to hurry back to the castle.

Grabbing up a bow dropped by a soldier in his efforts to escape her pet's snapping teeth, Odethia walked around to the back of the cottage. She notched the arrow, drew the bowstring taut and with a word of magic, let it fly straight into the sky toward the gathering clouds in the west. The arrow flew on straight and true until it was out of sight.

A moment later there was a tiny flash in the sky and the distant rumble of thunder. Odethia watched as the clouds began to expand, boiling higher and higher into the sky. She smiled slightly as the clouds quickly multiplied and began to darken menacingly. A wind began to blow, softly at first, building quickly to near gale force. A deep drumroll of thunder shook the cottage shutters and the sorceress cackled with glee. A jagged pitchfork of lightning crackled to the earth and the rains came.

The forest fire roared angrily as the rain began to battle it. Its roar became a growl and then just hissing like a small cat as it accepted its defeat.

"I <u>shall</u> have my revenge!" the sorceress shouted over the storm and she danced and laughed in the drenching downpour and growing puddles. She was still snickering as she finally turned and walked back into the cottage to stoke the fire and wait.

CHAPTER 16

Unseen in all the mayhem, Merrick had been able to make his way around the back of the cottage. He found the soldiers sent by Ruxton lying unconscious on the ground. He quickly roused them and sent them off in a direction that would skirt the battle.

When the dragon's fire exploded into a wall of flame, Merrick had found the back door, put a rock from the garden in his pocket and entered the kitchen area. He recognized the tools of the sorceress in the jars and hanging herbs.

He silently made his way through the sitting room and into the sleeping room. Here he would wait and prepare.

Feeling the urgency of her brother's plight, Krystin rode on. She was lost in her thoughts when suddenly there was a crashing of breaking branches above her. She jerked her head up in time to see the dragon descending recklessly above her. It landed awkwardly in the brush, shaking the ground.

Krystin's horse reared, throwing her off. She hit the ground hard, knocking the air out of her. She lay there dazed as her horse bolted off through the brush and trees with a frightened bellow.

She knew she must get up, but just trying to breathe was difficult enough. Finally Krystin raised herself up on her elbow and shook her head trying to clear her senses. She looked for her horse, but saw instead the dragon's fierce head, its startling blue eyes looking down at her. She felt its hot breath in her face, its huge front foot came down upon her chest, its claws digging into the ground on both sides of her, effectively trapping her. Krystin wanted to scream, but was too terrified until she realized this was no terrible beast! It was her brother! David wouldn't harm her, would he?

She reached out her hand to dragon. "David!" she cried. "David, it's me, Krystin!" The beast rumbled as it focused on its captive. It <u>was</u> a bit hungry.

"David!" she cried again. "It's Krystin, your sister! Please, listen to me!" Krystin's green eyes grew wide as her fear lurched anew in her chest.

Suddenly the dragon jerked its head up. *The green eyes!* It had expected the pain in its head to return when this creature spoke, but there was none. *"David!"* It heard that word again. Somehow familiar. But the green eyes. It was confusing.

Krystin was surprised as the dragon released her and stood back. It sat like a puppy and cocked its head sideways staring at her. She got up slowly and stood unsteadily before it.

"David! Can you understand me?" she tried again. Then as she looked upon the dragon she saw the arrow holes and sword wounds. "You're hurt!" she cried. "Let me help you."

Krystin ripped a part of her tunic off and stepped up to dab at the oozing wounds. The dragon rumbled as she approached, but remained still, wincing slightly at her touch. She began singing to soothe her brother as she had done when they were just children.

"Sleep, now sleep. Don't make a peep! Moonbeams will light your way! Take your dreams, while starlight gleams, fly to the skies and play!" Krystin sang the song again and again, over and over.

Somewhere deep in the dragon's mind, the song penetrated to the part that was still David. The melody surrounded the beast like cooling water. It felt safe and all anger drained away. It lay down its great body and closed its eyes. *Sleep, now sleep.* The dragon felt a gentle hand on its neck. *Sleep, now sleep.* It was so tired. *Sleep.*

The great dragon lay at Krystin's feet sleeping. She was elated! She had subdued the dragon! She would save her brother yet! But how to get him back to the castle and back to his human form? Merrick would surely know. He must know! But where was he? How could she reach him? For now she had to wait. She had her brother to watch over. And she was content with that for the moment.

As soon as he had hidden in the cottage, Merrick took the stone from his pocket. He began the complex spell, muttering the words ever so softly. It would take some time to complete. He hoped he would have enough time. His words continued as he heard the dragon roaring and the flames crackling through the trees. He heard the commander shout the retreat. Heard the dragon fly away.

Now he alone was left to deal with the sorceress.

Odethia rattled though her jars, and as he took a quick peek, she was tying a small packet onto an arrow and then, with a bow, she stepped out the back door. Several minutes later, the prince felt the change in the air due to the rising storm. Thunder rattled the jars and lightning briefly illuminated the cottage like a hundred candles, causing Merrick to flinch and nearly pause in his incantation.

Rain poured down on the roof and the fire protested its demise. Merrick listened to the wildly laughing sorceress and heard the door creak as she entered back into the kitchen. Merrick crouched low. The prince ducked away into the shadows of the bedroom, afraid of being detected too soon.

The sorceress hummed to herself as she built a fire in the sitting room to dry her hair and clothes. She made tea and lit candles, talking to herself about revenge and the stupidity of kings and kings' men. She laughed out loud.

Merrick's words went on and on; weaving his magical net in ever-increasing layers, as the last of the day's light was swallowed by the storm. The stone in his hand had begun to glow and he shielded its light with his cloak. He was beaded with sweat and could not afford to be discovered until the spell was complete.

This was his best plan to capture the sorceress. If this failed, he would have to fight her with magic and that would mean death for one of them. He was not sure he could deal with her powers of mind control. His own powers would require him to open his mind to hers and that would be dangerous. He had to keep her out of his mind to defeat her. He glanced down at the stone. It was beginning to look transparent like an illuminated crystal. Grinning slightly, he realized he was exhausted but nearly finished.

Odethia felt a tingling at the edge of her mind as she bent drying her hair in front of the hearth in the sitting room. Something was wrong. She listened. It was still raining. *That was good.* Thunder continued to roll off toward the castle. *That was good.*

She reached out her mind to the dragon. It was still flying toward the castle. *Fly on, my pet!* she urged it. She could sense her creature's weariness. If it slept now, perhaps it would be ready to deal with the soldiers again when they finally caught up. She would let it sleep if it wanted.

Her serpent had served her well so far. She didn't want the soldiers to kill her pet. At least not yet. Not until her revenge was complete. Then, as her enchantment over him weakened, she would abandon the dragon to its fate with the soldiers. She smiled wickedly at the thought.

The sorceress's eyes narrowed as she felt the tingling again. There was something with magical essence near by. Or someone. She stepped through the back door into the wet darkness outside and began to search with her mind the surrounding forest. *Nothing there but mundane creatures.*

Coming back into the kitchen, she closed the door, bolting it in place. *Could something among her herbs and potions be emitting a magical aura?* She checked through her things carefully. *Not there.*

The tingling got stronger. Odethia slowly swept the cottage with her mind. *There! There it was! In her sleeping room!* She felt it strongly now. *So close!* She crept toward the room and Merrick.

CHAPTER 17

Krystin's mind whirled with unanswered questions and unfinished plans. Hours had gone by and still the dragon that was her brother slept on. She had not been able to figure a way to get Merrick and the dragon together. She didn't have enough information. Where was Merrick? Who else could help her? How could she coax her brother to the castle and would that be safe for the people there? How would he react to them? Would the soldiers protect him or try to kill him? There seemed to be no answers.

Thunder rumbled off in the distance. A cold wind ruffled the trees above her. Krystin knew it was going to rain and soon it would be dark. *Oh, Krystin!* she thought to herself. *Now what will you do?* She really hadn't thought much past finding and helping her brother. Now that she had him, what could she do with him?

All at once she heard approaching sounds far off. The snapping of twigs under many heavy feet. Horses snorting and the scrunch of saddle leather. The soldiers were returning! And here lay the dragon in their path! Had Merrick gotten to them with her father's message? Had they captured the sorceress? Perhaps Merrick was with them now! Krystin's heart raced. This was the help she needed! *Think, Krystin! They mustn't startle the dragon before Merrick can come to help!*

Krystin waited. Should she run to them and risk losing her brother? No, she would wait. It was completely dark when she put her hand on the dragon's neck and began to sing as much to calm herself as for her brother. "Sleep, now sleep. Don't make a peep! Moonbeams will light your way! Take your dreams, while starlight gleams, fly to the skies and play!" She kept singing as the soldiers with their bobbing torches drew nearer and the noise increased. Krystin sang louder.

Suddenly the advancing men stopped. "Who goes there?" a voice rang out of the dark. Krystin could hear arrows being pulled from their quivers. "Identify yourself or we'll shoot!" They were still too far away to cast any light upon her and the quiet form behind her.

"Commander Ruxton!" Krystin shouted out. "It's Princess Krystin! Please don't shoot!"

"Princess? Is that really you? What are you doing out here? Are you alone?"

Krystin decided not to reveal the presence of the dragon just yet. She had to find out if Merrick had delivered his message first.

"Have you seen Prince Merrick? Is he with you? Did he give you the message from my father?" Krystin could see a couple of torches advancing slowly toward her now. In the torchlight she could make out Commander Ruxton's rough face flanked by two armed soldiers.

"Merrick is not here," Ruxton yelled back. Yellow torchlight flashed off the sword in his hand. "He ran off back at the cottage, the fool." He made no effort to hide the contempt in his voice.

"But did he deliver the king's message about the dragon?" Krystin still had to raise her voice to be heard.

"Message? Oh, yes, we got the message about not harming the sorceress or the dragon. And some nonsense about the dragon being Prince David? I'll have a word or two for His Highness about that when we get to the castle." The commander's eyes gazed steadily at Krystin and his look was not kindly.

Commander Ruxton had been fooled once already, and he was not about to be fooled again. Just what would the real princess be doing out in the forest alone at night? He had noticed something strange about this person who proclaimed she was the princess as soon as the light had come close enough to reveal her fully. First, she was certainly not dressed like a girl, let alone a princess, and second, there was a very odd looking rock behind her that appeared to be moving.

Krystin felt the dragon stir behind her. Her time was running out. "Commander Ruxton, you will please remember that order from the king when I tell you that I have my brother, David, here with me now. He has not hurt me. We must find Merrick and get him and my brother to the castle so that Merrick can change him back to his human form."

Ruxton stopped several yards from Krystin. He stood scowling at her. "You must really think me a fool!" he growled in a low voice. "I'm sure you'd like nothing better than for us to take that beast right into the castle! Do you think I'm stupid!" the old veteren yelled.

Krystin was so shocked she couldn't speak at first. "But Commander, how else shall we save my brother?"

"Oh, don't give me that innocent act again!" bellowed Ruxton. "I don't know how you got here ahead of us and I don't care. But we will take you along with us now!"

At this the dragon became fully awake and slowly raised up behind Krystin with rumbling in his throat.

Ruxton and his men scuttled back. "It's the sorceress and her winged serpent!" one of the men shouted.

"Defend yourselves, men!" shouted out the commander. "Archers, fire!"

Krystin was horrified. They were firing at her and her brother. She dove to the ground, while behind her the dragon roared and arrows rained down on him.

DANGER! The dragon's instincts took over. *HURT!* It wanted to get away. *DANGER!*

Looking up at the dragon, Krystin cried, "David! Help me!"

That voice! The dragon's mind cleared slightly. *That singing voice! What did it say to do? Fly to the skies? YES! FLY!* The dragon stepped over Krystin protectively and, picking her up in its front claws, spread its wings and launched itself into the night sky.

Krystin couldn't stifle her scream this time as she felt herself lifted off the ground and carried into the blackness of the night. The cries of the soldiers and the whizzing of arrows faded away below her as they rocketed straight up over the treetops. She clung to the dragon's foreleg, the cold air bringing tears to her eyes, as her breath came in gasps. Her mind was numb as she watched the dark forest below fall away and the stars loom nearer.

The dragon's strong wings carried them higher and higher. Suddenly, Krystin caught hold of an idea. *Hadn't her brother helped her escape the danger?* Perhaps she could yet direct him. "DAVID!' she yelled into the wind. "DAVID, TAKE ME HOME! TAKE ME HOME!"

HOME. HOME, said the singing voice. The dragon knew where home was. So did the David deep inside him. The dragon banked its wings and turned toward the south. It would take her home. Home was where a diamond window let in the moonlight.

CHAPTER 18

Merrick felt a sudden silence in the cottage. He knew his time was up. The sorceress had finally sensed his magic. It was a common thing among the people of his world as everyone possessed magic. Each person had their own magical feel. It seemed strange in this mundane world. Not feeling anyone. But now the sorceress had found him, and partly because of the increased magical field he generated with his spellcasting.

He muttered the final words of the spell he had been laboring over and the stone's light went out. He hurriedly put the stone back into his pocket, threw his cloak's hood over his head and prepared himself to shield his mind from the sorceress's prying eyes.

Odethia came to the sleeping room door. She stopped. The intensity of magic she had felt suddenly lessened. Like curtains being drawn over a sunlit window. *Strange.*

She mentally probed the deepening shadows, still seeking the exact source of the magic. When she had found it, she called out, "Come out, you! I know you are there!" She focused her eyes on the spot, hoping to enslave whoever it was immediately upon eye contact.

A dark, hunched figure rose from its hiding place. "Come out of there!" Odethia commanded. "Step into the light!" She backed away, never taking her eyes from the stranger, and slowly drew the figure into the brighter light of the sitting room.

Merrick kept his back bent and his head down, his face concealed in his hooded cloak, avoiding her gaze. He came creeping forward, inching his way to the sitting room. The sorceress watched him intently, content to let him move slowly.

When he finally stood before her with his back to the fire, she spoke.

"Who are you?" she demanded. "Why are you hiding in my house?"

Merrick remained silent, his head down. He had to wait for the right time to spring his trap. He had to be able to draw her near, to touch her without coming under her power.

"Look at me!" Odethia commanded him. "Look at me, I say!" But she kept her distance from him, uncertain about this mysterious figure.

Merrick had to make her feel confident and in control. He began to tremble, and feigning weakness sank down onto a bench. "I am ill," he croaked in a low voice. "I . . . I needed shelter. I meant no harm."

The sorceress was not easily swayed. She had felt a magical tug. There was something this person was hiding. She would play along for now. She had time. "Let me get you a warm drink," she said with a smile, backing toward the kitchen.

Krystin jerked awake. The wind whipped her hair away from her face as she sucked in a breath. Her feet dangled, and below her feet the world was rushing by. So far below! She must have fainted. Her ribs felt bruised from the dragon's grip around her. She had asked the dragon to take her home. She was hoping it would take her to the castle, but that was obviously not what the David-dragon had in mind.

She felt the movement of the massive wings above her change. Her stomach lurched with a sudden drop in altitude as they entered a cloud. Water droplets clung to her face, hair and clothes until she felt quite damp and cold. She shivered uncontrollably in the rushing wind.

The dragon continued to descend through the clouds and into the rainy night sky below. Krystin was soaked to the skin by then. She could see nothing in the blackness as she hung helpless in the dragon's clutch. Then all at once the ground appeared, coming up too fast beneath them. Krystin gasped and felt faint. Then she saw a familiar looking glow as the dragon dropped heavily to the earth. Her body jerked with the impact but was cushioned somewhat by the dragon. It shook the excess water from its scales and folded back its wings.

The beast set its shivering singer on the ground in front of the warmly glowing windows of the forest cottage. It was home.

Odethia wanted to scream with frustration. What she thought was going to be an amusing diversion had turned into an ordeal. No matter what she did, this man, this intruder, had resisted her every effort to gain some information or control over his mind.

She had offered him a drugged herb drink to loosen his tongue. He had convulsed into a fit of coughing and refused to drink it. She had offered to take his cloak, but he only clung tighter to it. She could not make contact with his eyes deep in the shadows of his hood.

The sorceress had tried to see into his mind but it seemed quite empty of any coherent thought. It was almost as if he knew her very powers! He was either very clever or the brainless wart he appeared to be.

And there still had been that tingle of magic. She knew she had felt it. Perhaps it was some talisman he carried. Some charm imbued with magic. She questioned him extensively, but was mostly answered by grunts and shrugs. The sorceress was growing angry and impatient with her guest. She should just turn him out into the night and be done with him.

She no longer felt threatened by his presence. He seemed only to want to sit by the fire and nap. Her curiosity was unsatisfied but she could waste no more time on him. She needed to concentrate on continuing her plans for Zarcon's revenge.

There was a sudden ground shaking thud outside the cottage, like a large tree falling to the earth. The sorceress smiled. Her pet had returned. Perhaps this would help her visitor either talk or leave. She went to the door and opened it.

Windswept rain swirled in and Odethia lifted her arm to shield her face. When she put her arm down, there stood a drenched young woman close to her same age, shivering and looking longingly at the warm fire within. "It seems to be the night for visitors," the sorceress said mostly to herself. She stood aside and motioned the girl into the room.

The dragon lay quietly outside, edging toward sleep again. Odethia sent a burning thought into its mind. It felt her painful green eyes and roared, shaking its head to free itself of the hurt. "I'll deal with you later!" the sorceress promised, closing the door.

CHAPTER 19

Merrick secretly glanced up as Krystin entered the room. *Oh, no!* he thought. *Where had she come from? What was she doing here?* This was a complication he hadn't forseen. Krystin would not be able to fend off the sorceress's mental probes. She would be in danger and he might be revealed for who he was. His plan could be ruined. He had to act quickly yet carefully.

He anxiously waited as Odethia got Krystin into dry clothes, seated her in the sitting room and was in the kitchen preparing her a <u>special</u> cup of tea. Merrick kept his head down when the sorceress was near, but now he chanced another quick glance at Krystin.

Krystin had not noticed the hunched figured wrapped in a cloak by the fire. But now she felt eyes upon her and turned. The hood turned away and Krystin eyed the figure curiously. She could not see the face under the hood but felt sure whoever it was had been looking at her. *Could this be the sorceress?* Perhaps this beautiful red-haired girl was her servant, poor thing.

Memories of Zarcon's evil face surfaced in Krystin's mind. Certainly a sorceress who was filled with such wickedness could have little beauty. It would not be surprising that she would hide beneath a cloak.

Krystin was unsure of what to do. But she knew she could be in great danger if the sorceress discovered who she was. She would have to be careful. She kept her distance from the hooded figure and never turned her back on it.

Where could Merrick be? What was he doing? Had he returned to the castle? That thought terrified her and she shivered involuntarily.

Odethia handed Krystin a warm cup of tea which she gratefully wrapped her cold hands around. As she raised it to her lips, the hooded figure began to cough uncontrollably. Startled, Krystin gasped in fear instead of sipping the tea.

"Who is that?" Krystin whispered to Odethia.

"Don't worry," Odethia replied sweetly. "It's just some old codger that I found hiding in the cottage. He's ill but harmless, and," she raised her voice so Merrick could hear, "I'm sure he will be leaving soon." She smiled at Krystin. "I'm Odethia." The sorceress narrowed her green eyes at Kristen. "And what did you say your name was?"

"I . . . I . . . ," Krystin stammered.

"Never mind, my sweet," Odethia looked deep into Krystin's eyes. "Just drink your tea and then you can tell me <u>all</u> about it."

"Thank you," Krystin sighed as she looked into Odethia's remarkable green eyes. Krystin felt herself drawn into those eyes. There were so beautiful. All her own will drained from her and she was powerless to turn aside her gaze. She felt her arms raise the cup to her mouth, tipping it gently to her lips. The tea was warm and soothing. She swallowed and Krystin felt her fears melting.

"That's right. Drink some more." Krystin could hear Odethia's voice, but it seemed to be coming from so far away. "Everything is all right now."

Merrick cringed, feeling powerless as he watched Krystin drink the tea he knew was drugged. His time was running out.

He had to get close to the sorceress. Close enough to grab her and hold on while he invoked his spell to capture her.

Odethia stood glaring menacingly at Krystin. "Now, my sweet, you <u>will</u> tell me who you are!"

"Yes," sighed Krystin dreamily. She looked up at Odethia. "I'm Princess Krystin of Lyndell, daughter of King Stephon and Queen Aryanne." Krystin had never had a real best friend before, but now she felt Odethia could certainly be that friend. She wanted to tell her everything. All her dreams and deepest secrets. And so she began to do just that.

After a few moments of Krystin's ramblings about the wonders of castle life, Krystin stopped and smiled. "And guess what?" she exclaimed. "I'm in love with a prince!"

Over near the fire, Merrick choked and started coughing. *Is it me?* he thought. *Could she love me?*

Odethia's eyes were full of hatred as she burst out, "So <u>you</u> are the one who killed Zarcon!"

Krystin, under the influence of the tea, could sense none of the anger that was being directed at her. "Oh, no!" she replied innocently. "It was Glurb, protector of the swamp, who ate Zarcon."

Odethia screamed again. She clenched her fists and began to stomp her feet in a fit of rage. All the while Krystin sat peacefully smiling, with the cup of tea in her hands.

"I'll boil you alive!" Odethia shrieked. "I'll turn you into a fly and pluck off your wings and legs one at a time! I'll . . . I'll . . ."

All at once Odethia stood deadly still and quiet. A most evil grin slowly creased her face. Turning back toward Krystin, she began to giggle. "Oh, no. None of that for a princess!" The sorceress's voice was low and sickening sweet. "I have just the thing! Oh, how delicious! How perfectly wonderful your death will be!"

The sorceress sent urgent thoughts out to the sleeping dragon. *Come help me, my pet! I'm in danger! Come NOW! DANGER!*

The dragon was instantly awake. The green eyes were burning painfully in its mind. *DANGER!* It got up and moved toward the cottage.

The sorceress moved closer to Krystin. She ran her forefinger down the side of Krystin's face, all the while giggling wickedly. "Oh, how Zarcon would have loved the sweetness of his revenge! The princess killed by her own brother who is a dragon, who will in turn be killed by his own parents!" She threw her head back and squawked out a laugh.

"Come, my dear! There's someone coming you'll be <u>dying</u> to meet!" The sorceress took Krystin by the hand and began to lead her toward the cottage door.

Suddenly the door burst apart and the dragon's head and neck came roaring into the room. The door frame heaved as the creature tried to get its body through, one front leg was pinned between the frame and its body. It raked the floor with its claws, splintering the wooden planks, roaring with the anguish in its mind.

The sorceress sent a searing command to her serpent. *KILL HER!*

The cloaked figure was immediately on his feet, lurching toward Krystin, feigning a ragged cough as he staggered forward. Odethia's attention was riveted on the dragon. Krystin turned an instant before the strange figure crashed into her, knocking her to the floor and away from the dragon.

"You old fool!" shrieked the sorceress. "Get out! Get out of here now!" she reached to shove him toward the door. "The dragon can eat you as well!" *KILL THEM BOTH!*

Merrick knew this was his only chance. He grabbed Odethia's arm as if to steady himself, and pulled her closer to him but stepped away from the dragon's snapping jaws. She resisted, trying to free herself of his grasp.

"Let go of me!" the sorceress screeched and began to strike him. Merrick drew out the crystallized rock he had prepared and immediately lifted his head, looking straight into the sorceress' face.

Her shock at seeing a young man under the hood and one that she recognized as well was just the moment Merrick needed to thrust the stone between their gazes. Odethia's eyes were automatically drawn to the crystal. She gasped and realized too late what it was as Merrick spoke the words of power.

"NO!" she screamed. "NOOOooooo!" her word was drawn out as her form became rubbery and elastic. She stretched and twisted, the enchanted capturing stone sucking her inside itself. But Odethia would not give up. She sent her thoughts to the dragon. *Help me! DANGER! DANGER!*

Krystin wasn't sure what was happening. She had been forcefully thrown to the floor, her breath knocked out of her. Now Krystin cowered away as Odethia screamed, not sure what was happening or who was the most dangerous.

The hooded figure did not release his hold on Odethia as the dragon snapped its jaws at him, roaring ferociously at the pain in its mind.

Krystin! Krystin, listen to me!

Krystin was hearing a voice in her head. *You must control your brother!* Her eyes turned toward the dragon, trying to understand. *That voice! Those words! It was Merrick!* He was here somewhere.

Her mind was foggy. She felt like she was just waking up from a dream. Again she heard his pleading voice.

Krystin! Help me! I can do nothing until the imprisoning spell is complete.

Krystin got up stiffly. Everything seemed to be moving in slow motion. She stood to face her brother, calling out his name weakly.

"David! It's me, Krystin!" The dragon continued to claw and snap at the figure holding tightly to Odethia as she writhed and contorted in his grasp.

"Stop! Stop!" Krystin cried louder to her brother. The dragon could only feel the pain in its mind. DANGER! It wanted the pain to stop.

The door frame began to creak and crack under the dragon's continuous force. In another second the creature would be able to close its jaws around what it thought was the cause of its pain.

Then Krystin began to sing. Softly at first, then louder and louder to match the dragon's agonized roaring and Odethia's screeching struggles against the powerful magic of the stone.

The dragon felt the song before hearing it. Like a gentle breeze cooling and caressing his mind. The beast stopped roaring and turned toward Krystin. The sorceress again sent a stabbing command into the dragon's mind. *KILL HER!*

The pain! No! Stop the pain! The dragon roared once more, but Krystin never faltered in her song. The dragon turned toward

Krystin and opened its mind to her singing, to let the song in and stop the burning pain of those green eyes. It welcomed the song. It was calming. The dragon began to grow quieter. The pain was fading, the eyes withdrawing down a long dark tunnel, spinning slowly away.

"You will pay for your treacheryyyyyyyyyyyyyyyyyyy!" The sorceress's threatening voice grew faint as she finally disappeared completely within the stone.

The dragon let the music wash over its mind. The beast felt heavy and sleepy. It let itself down in the doorway as the pain subsided and the feelings of danger vanished.

Krystin's song faded to a whisper and then ceased altogether. All at once the cottage was quiet and still.

CHAPTER 20

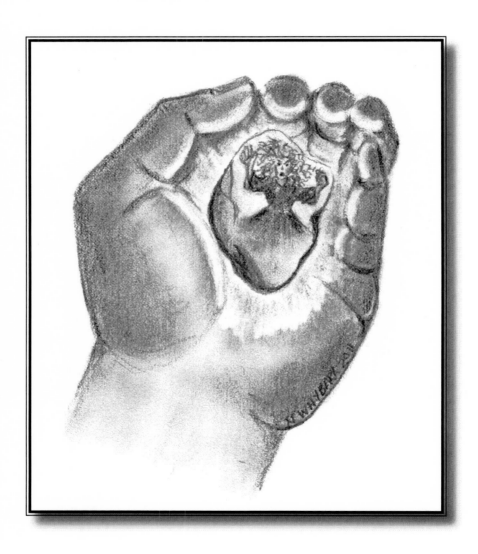

Merrick threw back the cloak's hood and whirled to face Krystin. "Well done!" he cried. "I thought for a moment there I was to become intimately acquainted with your brother's teeth!"

She stood with her mouth gaping open still in shock over what had just happened. "You . . . she . . . I . . ." Krystin muttered, shaking all over.

Crossing the room with quick strides, Merrick put his arms around Krystin to comfort her. After a few minutes he drew away and held the crystallized stone up for her to see.

There, to Krystin's astonishment, was a very tiny Odethia ranting and raving inside her glowing prison. The sorceress's mouth was moving but no sound could be heard as she pounded on the walls that surrounded her.

"Will she have to stay in there forever?" Krystin asked, still feeling some of the effects of the tea.

"No," Merrick replied. "The spell is temporary, but will give me time to take her back for punishment for her crimes on both our worlds."

The dragon stirred and rumbled in its sleep and Krystin flinched nervously. "What about my brother? Can you change him back?" she asked anxiously.

Merrick shook his head. "I'm afraid that is going to take a while longer. And you will have to do much of it."

"Me?" cried Krystin. "What do I know of magic and potions?"

Merrick briefly explained to Krystin that he would teach her how to make the antidote potion to reverse Odethia's enchantments upon her brother. It would take several days and perhaps as much as a week for David to regain his human form. It was important that during that time someone stay close to him and watch over him. Merrick thought Krystin seemed to be the best choice for the task.

"Of course I'll do it!" Krystin confirmed when Merrick had finished his explanation. "Besides, I wouldn't want anyone else to. He is <u>my</u> brother."

"Very well then," said Merrick smiling. "Let's start right now."

Slipping the stone in his pocket, he escorted Krystin to the kitchen and began to explain to her how to mix the antidote.

Krystin had learned how to cook long ago in this very same kitchen, but now it all seemed so new and strange with all the herbs and jars. But she was an apt learner and quickly was able to duplicate Merrick's recipe. Now came the task of getting the dragon to drink it!

After a few fumbling attempts and several spilled batches, the dragon finally was able to lap up the potion. It seemed to actually like the taste!

Merrick decided Krystin was equal to the task and so, after mentally summoning his horse that had fled into the forest, left right away to let King Stephon know that his children were safe and that the sorceress, along with her dragon, was contained. After which he would return to Irth, his own world, taking Odethia for judgment.

Krystin looked longingly after the prince as he rode away. She wondered if she would ever see him again.

By the second day of antidote potions, Krystin began to notice small changes in her brother's appearance. He was getting smaller for one thing. He could now fit in the sitting room easily. His tail was shrinking and the ridges down his spine were no more than large bumps. Krystin chatted to him constantly. Reassuring him that all would be well. She stroked his head and sang to him often.

Soldiers on horseback came riding in on the afternoon of the fifth day. Merrick had indeed delivered the message to the king, who had sent the soldiers at the queen's insistence. They brought extra food and supplies along with horses for Krystin and David when the time came for them to return to the castle. The soldiers fixed a temporary door for the cottage and camped outside as watchful protection.

By the sixth day, David had reappeared. No longer a dragon in any way physically, his sister moved him to the loft bedroom. But his mind was still somewhat fogged, his thoughts and speech difficult. Krystin was a patient nurse and talked each day about their childhood, recounting all that had happened to their family. Then she began to tell him about the sorceress and his own enchantment, and how Merrick had come and saved them all. At night she sang him to sleep in the loft, and then crept to her own little bed, often too exhausted to sleep right away.

On the morning of the eighth day, David shook Krystin awake. Her eyes slowly opened as she tried to focus on the blurry figure leaning over her. She rubbed her eyes.

"Come on, sleepy head!" she heard David's cheerful voice call out. Krystin sat up in bed.

"David! You sound better! Are you all right?" David smiled at her warmly as he gently grasped her hand.

"Let's go home," he said.

It didn't take them long to pack what they needed for the journey to the castle. They'd traveled this way together before. But now instead of heading toward the unknown, they were going home and they knew the way well. They couldn't convince the soldiers to leave them as they had received strict commands from the king and queen to escort the pair back to the castle. So they gave in and trotted along through the woods with their overseers.

The trip was uneventful, which suited all the travelers just fine after recent happenings. When they reached the forest edge, David pulled up his mount as Krystin came along side him. They gazed out at the open meadow before them and the gleaming castle spires touched by the lowering afternoon sun.

It seemed a lifetime ago since David had first laid eyes on this scene. He had done a lot of growing up in the last few years, but now he felt he was turning toward manhood. Somehow being a dragon, a wild, untamed creature, had calmed some of the wildness within him. Perhaps now he was ready to take on his duties as prince. Perhaps. David took a deep breath and smiled.

"It really is good to be back," he said quietly.

"It's good to have you back," his sister replied, gazing at him. Then David's grin widened.

"Race you!" he called as he kicked his horse to a run.

Krystin shouted after him as she flicked her horse with her reins. The two thundered through the meadow and over the drawbridge at a full gallop. The guards on the bridge cursed as they dove out of the way, an unlucky one tripping into the moat.

The crowd scattered before the galloping pair, side by side. Villagers shrieked as dogs barked and a cart overturned sending its contents flying.

Willier looked out from an upper window in the royal quarters hearing the uproar Krystin and David's arrival had caused in the main courtyard. "The young prince has returned with his sister," he announced to the king and queen. "And he seems to be in very good health," he added smiling.

CHAPTER 21

"Y ou're trying to kill me, aren't you!" Queen Aryanne turned to face her husband.

"Of course not, dear. You know how much it will help our child grow and gain new experiences. It will be wonderful."

"But it's so far away."

"It won't be forever."

"And all that strange magic."

"Our child will have a capable tutor and guardian."

"But what if . . ."

Stephon embraced the queen. "We could talk about 'what ifs' all day. Don't worry. All will be well."

Krystin had been eavesdropping again. She heard her parents moving toward the door and hurried away. She had heard enough though to start her heart thumping. Could it be <u>her</u> they were talking about? She was being sent away to Irth! How she hoped that tutor would be Merrick. Who else would her father trust there? It had to be him. This would be the greatest adventure yet. A whole other world to explore!

Krystin ran to her room to dress for court. The day's business would soon be starting and she wanted to look her best when her father announced her departure. *Merrick could be coming today as well,* she thought suddenly. She breathed a sigh as her heart beat a little faster. She hadn't seen Merrick since that day he had captured Odethia. He had returned to Irth several weeks ago and there had been no word from him.

Just as Krystin had expected, a courtier knocked on her door with the message that her presence was requested in the throne room for a special announcement. Krystin wanted to run all the way there, but restrained herself to a stiff, quick stride. She found many of the court dignitaries already present as well as David and her mother. Willier stood smiling next to her father, who was traditionally seated on the throne with his queen next to him.

When Krystin was seated next to David, King Stephon rose and said, "Today will mark a new age for Lyndell. We have established communication with another world far beyond our own and yet so very close. We are going to send an ambassador to this world called Irth. I have chosen one of my own children to take on this responsibility."

Krystin's eyes had been scanning the crowd. She had noticed the rear doors open and close but could not see who had entered for all the people standing around. But her attention was drawn back to her father at his last words. She smiled brightly, waiting expectantly for him to announce that she had been chosen.

The king went on. "Of course it will not be Prince Eron. As crown prince he is needed here. I have chosen . . . ."

A hush fell over the court. King Stephon stopped mid-sentence. His eyes narrowed as he gazed toward the back of the room. Then he smiled and nodded.

"But first, I think it might be appropriate for you all to meet the ambassador from the Realm of en'Edlia on this new world. Come forward, Merrick, son of High Patriarch Brokt and High Matriarch Narrian and crown prince to the throne of that realm.

The crowd respectfully parted as Merrick strode forward to the throne. He looked every bit a prince now in a rich, green velvet coat embroidered with gold designs. His black pants were neatly tucked into his black, shiny knee boots, which had gold-buckled straps at the ankles. He wore a medal around his neck on a wide, purple and yellow satin ribbon. There was a glint of gold on his forehead.

Krystin clasped her hands tightly together and tried to keep still and remain in her seat as was expected of a dignified princess, soon to be ambassador. She blushed and lowered her eyes as Merrick gave her a wink in passing.

Merrick bowed low before King Stephon. "Your Highness! It is good to see you again. My father, High Patriarch Brokt, sends his greetings and approval of our exchange of ambassadors. He has sent gifts of his good will." Merrick clapped his hands and four chests appeared at his feet.

The crowd gasped and drew back in fear, but the king stepped forward and spoke. "Good people, do not fear! Prince Merrick comes from a place where such feats are commonplace. He is not evil, as was the wizard, Zarcon. He has proven his trust by saving my son, Prince David, from the spells of a sorceress. We can only become stronger by learning more of his world and people and by exchanging goods and services with them."

"Thank you, Your Highness!" said Merrick, bowing again. Then he knelt and opened the chests. The gasps of wonder rippled through the throne room as the people saw that three chests were filled with gems and jewels the size and colors of which were never seen before, as well as strange shiny shells and treasures from the sea. These Merrick had to explain as those of Lyndell had never before seen the sea.

The opening of the fourth chest released a creature that flew into the air. Ladies screamed and even the guards ducked as it circled over head. Krystin could not help emitting a cry at the sight of such a thing.

Whistling for it, the creature came to Merrick and landed on his forearm, clutching his leather-covered sleeve with delicate claws. Its glittering green eyes looked at the king as it folded its leathery wings on its back. Its snake-like tail hung down a foot and its body was pale green and scaly with brown, triangular markings on its sides.

The king had pushed himself back onto his throne. His face was stern. "What? Have you brought further destruction upon us? Is this not a dragon?"

Merrick smiled. "No, Your Highness. I brought this to honor your bravery and willingness to unite our worlds. This small creature looks like a dragon, but it will never grow any larger. It is called a firedrake. It is quite tame and no more harmful than a cat. It is a magnificent hunter of small game and can ignite the wettest wood on the coldest nights. It responds to whistles and is yours to command. Consider it as you would a trained falcon or hawk."

Stephon stood then and came forward hesitantly to inspect this strange gift. He carefully stroked the spiny head of the firedrake as Merrick instructed him, and soon had the little creature thrumming contentedly.

The king laughed then and slapped Merrick on the back. "Very well then, Ambassador Merrick! Your gifts are accepted and well met!" The two men turned to face the court again.

King Stephon's voice rose above all the chattering of the crowd. "Now I wish to announce Lyndell's ambassador to en'Edlia!"

When the room had quieted he continued. "This has been are hard decision for the queen and me and our advisors, but we feel it is a good one. So I call upon you, citizens of Lyndell, to give your support to . . ."

Krystin scooted to the edge of her chair and got ready to stand. She'd be the first woman ambassador of Lyndell.

". . . our first off-world ambassador, Prince David!"

David and Krystin both stood up in shock as the applause echoed around the room. They turned to each other blinking with disbelief. "I thought it was you!" David whispered to Krystin.

"Me too!" Krystin whispered back. Then she smiled and hugged her brother warmly. "You'll do fine." She brushed away a tear. She felt confused and couldn't tell if she was crying for the loss of her brother again so soon after getting him back, or for the disappointment at not being chosen herself.

David advanced to the throne and bowed to both his father and Prince Merrick. Willier handed the king a small box from which he drew out a medallion with the red, black and silver crest of Lyndell upon it.

"Ambassador David of Lyndell, go forth on your assignment with honor, dignity, loyalty and respect. Learn all you can, help where needed, and serve always. Let others see by your actions the quality of people we are here in Lyndell."

The king then placed the medallion around David's neck and proudly embraced him as the queen wept. David turned to the throng of people and waved while applause and cheering erupted again.

Krystin noticed that Merrick was whispering something in her father's ear. She got a strange feeling when her father looked right at her and smiled, then nodded to Merrick.

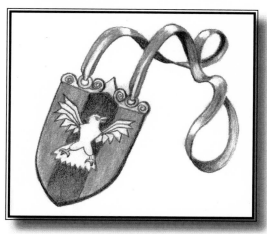

CHAPTER 22

The rest of the morning's business was postponed and the royal family along with Willier and Ambassador Merrick met in the chambers behind the throne room.

"David will not be leaving for another two weeks," explained Stephon, "as I will be instructing him on the finer points of ambassadorship and Merrick will be teaching him about the customs of his people. He has much to learn." The king paused to smile at his son.

"Then Merrick will accompany David to Irth for two more weeks to help him get settled. He'll be staying at the palace in en'Edlia with Merrick's family. After that Merrick will return here as ambassador on temporary assignment."

"Temporary assignment?" questioned David.

"Yes," explained the king, "you remember that Merrick is the crown prince and as such has certain responsibilities at home. He could be called home at any time if his father should be unable to continue as High Patriarch. So he is here only until his younger brother, Jarrius, is old enough for a . . . ," Stephon paused. "What was that again?"

"A quest," Merrick answered, smiling.

The queen, still looking a bit anxious over the whole thing, pleaded, "Couldn't we have Merrick's family here for a few days before David goes?"

"I think that might be arranged," commented Merrick. "I'll check in with my father as soon as I can, Your Highness."

"Thank you, Merrick," Aryanne replied warmly. "It would help me be more at ease actually meeting the people my son will be with."

"I'm sure my mother will understand and talk my father into it," Merrick said smiling. Then he turned to the king and said, "Wasn't there one more thing you wanted to announce, Your Highness?"

King Stephon chuckled, coughed, and then grew very serious. "Yes, you're quite right, Ambassador," he said formally. He turned toward his family and squared his shoulders, standing straight and tall. "It is my extreme privilege to announce that Prince Merrick, Ambassador of en'Edlia, has asked my permission to court our daughter, Princess Krystin, as a prelude to marriage."

The queen's hands flew to her mouth; a happy gasp escaped her smiling lips. David took hold of the chair he was standing next to. "Well, I'll be a sorceress's serpent," was all he could say.

Willier was bobbing his head with satisfaction, as Krystin collapsed in stunned silence on the chair David held.

The king, still looking serious and regal, turned his gaze upon Krystin. "I have given Merrick my permission, but what say you, my daughter? Will you consider this man to be your betrothed?"

Krystin looked up at her father, then at her mother. Could this be happening to her? She looked over at Merrick who was staring at her anxiously waiting for her answer. *Did she love him? Could she marry him?*

Time seemed to stand still as she considered these questions. Hadn't she dreamed of this moment? Yet now she felt timid in the face of yet another unknown adventure. She had faced an evil wizard and defeated him. She had tamed a dragon. Could she defeat her fears and tame her doubts one more time? She bit her lip and looked back into her father's smiling face.

"Yes," she said, her eyes sparkling. "I will."